Ragman

BOOKS BY WALTER WANGERIN JR.

The Book of God: The Bible as a Novel

Paul: A Novel

The Book of the Dun Cow

The Book of Sorrows

Preparing for Jesus

Reliving the Passion

Little Lamb, Who Made Thee?

The Manger Is Empty

Miz Lil and the Chronicles of Grace

Mourning into Dancing

The Orphean Passages

Ragman and Other Cries of Faith

Whole Prayer

In the Days of the Angels

As for Me and My House

The Crying for a Vision

Saint Julian

This Earthly Pilgrimage

Ragman

and other cries of faith

REVISED AND UPDATED
WITH 11 NEW STORIES

Walter Wangerin Jr.

HarperOne
An Imprint of HarperCollinsPublishers

HarperOne

Acknowledgment is made for permission to excerpt from "The Creation" from
God's Trombones by James Weldon Johnson. Copyright 1927 by The Viking
Press, Inc. Copyright renewed 1955 by Grace Nail Johnson. Reprinted by per-
mission of Viking Penguin, Inc.

Portions of this work originally appeared in somewhat different form in *Chris-
tianity Today*, *Leadership*, and *The Evansville Courier*.

HarperCollins books may be purchased for educational, business, or sales
promotional use. For information, please e-mail the Special Markets Department
at SPsales@harpercollins.com.

HarperCollins Web site: http://www.harpercollins.com

HarperCollins®, 👑®, and HarperOne™ are trademarks of
HarperCollins Publishers.

FIRST HARPERCOLLINS PAPERBACK EDITION PUBLISHED IN 1994

Library of Congress Cataloging-in-Publication Data

    Wangerin, Walter.
      Ragman and Other Cries of Faith.
      ISBN 978–0–06–052614–6
      1. Story-telling (Christian theology) I. Title.
BT78.W22   1984   230   83–48980

HB 08.19.2021

To Grace,
my joy
and several kinds of crowns to me

Contents

An Invocation

UNTO YOU, LORD. Unto you, Lord God of the Worlds, I turn. And even when I do not know that I am turning, I turn to you.

Your print is everywhere, and everywhere divine.

Where can I look and I do not see you?

Into myself? But I encompass you, who compass me from every corner, for I am sin and you forgiveness and I cannot live except it be by you. My life itself is yours. No, when I look at me I see the thing that you have done.

Then where can I look and I do not see you?

The city? Hot with human enmity, cold with old mortality, the city? Busy and fatigued; kissing below back alley stairs, lips as limp as rotten violets; and children cursing like their parents, parents careless; parties for wasted wealth on Saturday night, exhausted Sunday morning; cars and lights and sirens; ointments, rouges, polishes, colognes, and coin—the city? Turning to the city, do I turn from you?

No, my Lord, for you are in the city. In all the affairs of humankind, you are there. You were not ashamed to be born of a woman, flesh like hers and mine, troubled as she and I by all the bruises of that flesh. You emptied yourself to enter the city, and though your coming may not make it good, it makes you cry, and there you are. In the oily streets, damp with rain and human sin, lit by a single light, I see your face reflected. O God, your incarnation's in the streets. I see the city, and I cannot help but see you.

And I love you.

They ask me, "Whom do you love?" And I tell them I love you.

They ask, "But whom do you love?" I point to the city.

They insist, "But *whom* do you love?"

And since they cannot see you for themselves, I do the next best thing: I tell them stories. I tell them a thousand stories, Lord. For the city is active, and you are acting in it, always; and activity's a story. I tell them about you by telling them the story.

Some of the stories I fashion myself, pleading your patience with my poor imagination and praying it be righteous to shape your truth into a fiction. But others happened to me truly, through your grace; and I hope the people realize that what is mine is theirs by virtue of your universal presence. Convince them of your love, O Lord. And I use the forms they understand: drama, poetry and essay, fable, letters, memoirs, any form whereby the words may cry the Word. And I make it a book, that the city might take it deep into itself, home, home to its heart.

Because I love you, and I love them, too. But yours is the mightier love, and I wish they knew it. Oh! I wish they could laugh out loud for the knowledge of your love for them.

So I turn to you, here at the beginning:

Give them eyes, bright God, to see you everywhere. They *are* the city: to see you in themselves! Give them ears, thou roll of thunder, and feeling for your presence—in this book because I love you, in the streets because you choose to love them.

And since I am assured that faithful praying finds a faithful answer:

Gratias tibi Domine.
Advent, 1983

——•◆•——

PART ONE

The Christ of God

Ragman

I SAW A STRANGE SIGHT. I stumbled upon a story most strange, like nothing my life, my street sense, my sly tongue had ever prepared me for.

Hush, child. Hush, now, and I will tell it to you.

———◆———

Even before the dawn one Friday morning I noticed a young man, handsome and strong, walking the alleys of our City. He was pulling an old cart filled with clothes both bright and new, and he was calling in a clear, tenor voice: "Rags!" Ah, the air was foul and the first light filthy to be crossed by such sweet music.

"Rags! New rags for old! I take your tired rags! Rags!"

"Now, this is a wonder," I thought to myself, for the man stood six feet four, and his arms were like tree limbs, hard and muscular, and his eyes flashed intelligence. Could he find no better job than this, to be a ragman in the inner city?

I followed him. My curiosity drove me. And I wasn't disappointed.

Soon the Ragman saw a woman sitting on her back porch. She was sobbing into a handkerchief, sighing, and shedding a thousand tears. Her knees and elbows made a sad X. Her shoulders shook. Her heart was breaking.

The Ragman stopped his cart. Quietly, he walked to the woman, stepping round tin cans, dead toys, and Pampers.

"Give me your rag," he said so gently, "and I'll give you another."

He slipped the handkerchief from her eyes. She looked up, and he laid across her palm a linen cloth so clean and new that it shined. She blinked from the gift to the giver.

Then, as he began to pull his cart again, the Ragman did a strange thing: he put her stained handkerchief to his own face; and then *he* began to weep, to sob as grievously as she had done, his shoulders shaking. Yet she was left without a tear.

"This *is* a wonder," I breathed to myself, and I followed the sobbing Ragman like a child who cannot turn away from mystery.

"Rags! Rags! New rags for old!"

In a little while, when the sky showed grey behind the rooftops and I could see the shredded curtains hanging out black windows, the Ragman came upon a girl whose head was wrapped in a bandage, whose eyes were empty. Blood soaked her bandage. A single line of blood ran down her cheek.

Now the tall Ragman looked upon this child with pity, and he drew a lovely yellow bonnet from his cart.

"Give me your rag," he said, tracing his own line on her cheek, "and I'll give you mine."

The child could only gaze at him while he loosened the bandage, removed it, and tied it to his own head. The bonnet he set on hers. And I gasped at what I saw: for with the bandage went the wound! Against his brow it ran a darker, more substantial blood—his own!

"Rags! Rags! I take old rags!" cried the sobbing, bleeding, strong, intelligent Ragman.

The sun hurt both the sky, now, and my eyes; the Ragman seemed more and more to hurry.

"Are you going to work?" he asked a man who leaned against a telephone pole. The man shook his head.

The Ragman pressed him: "Do you have a job?"

"Are you crazy?" sneered the other. He pulled away from the

pole, revealing the right sleeve of his jacket—flat, the cuff stuffed into the pocket. He had no arm.

"So," said the Ragman. "Give me your jacket, and I'll give you mine."

Such quiet authority in his voice!

The one-armed man took off his jacket. So did the Ragman—and I trembled at what I saw: for the Ragman's arm stayed in its sleeve, and when the other put it on he had two good arms, thick as tree limbs; but the Ragman had only one.

"Go to work," he said.

After that he found a drunk, lying unconscious beneath an army blanket, an old man, hunched, wizened, and sick. He took that blanket and wrapped it round himself, but for the drunk he left new clothes.

———◆———

And now I had to run to keep up with the Ragman. Though he was weeping uncontrollably, and bleeding freely at the forehead, pulling his cart with one arm, stumbling for drunkenness, falling again and again, exhausted, old, old, and sick, yet he went with terrible speed. On spider's legs he skittered through the alleys of the City, this mile and the next, until he came to its limits, and then he rushed beyond.

I wept to see the change in this man. I hurt to see his sorrow. And yet I needed to see where he was going in such haste, perhaps to know what drove him so.

The little old Ragman—he came to a landfill. He came to the garbage pits. And then I wanted to help him in what he did, but I hung back, hiding. He climbed a hill. With tormented labor he cleared a little space on that hill. Then he sighed. He lay down. He pillowed his head on a handkerchief and a jacket. He covered his bones with an army blanket. And he died.

Oh, how I cried to witness that death! I slumped in a junked car and wailed and mourned as one who has no hope—because I had come to love the Ragman. Every other face had faded in the wonder of this man, and I cherished him; but he died. I sobbed myself to sleep.

I did not know—how could I know?—that I slept through Friday night and Saturday and its night, too.

But then, on Sunday morning, I was wakened by a violence.

Light—pure, hard, demanding light—slammed against my sour face, and I blinked, and I looked, and I saw the last and the first wonder of all. There was the Ragman, folding the blanket most carefully, a scar on his forehead, but alive! And, besides that, healthy! There was no sign of sorrow nor of age, and all the rags that he had gathered shined for cleanliness.

Well, then I lowered my head and, trembling for all that I had seen, I myself walked up to the Ragman. I told him my name with shame, for I was a sorry figure next to him. Then I took off all my clothes in that place, and I said to him with dear yearning in my voice: "Dress me."

He dressed me. My Lord, he put new rags on me, and I am a wonder beside him. The Ragman, the Ragman, the Christ!

Meditation on a New Year's Day

MIGHTY GOD!

Creator unbegun, unending!

Your works, when I think that they are yours, dazzle me to silence and to awe and aweful prayer.

For I am thrice removed from the knowledge of them, and each remove diminishes me until I am near nothing by your greatness. Yet you love me.

For I may know some little something of the sun, may take its temperature, may track its travels relative to other stars, may date its age, predict its death, observe the windy rage of its digestion in the time between. But what do such solar figures do to the size of me? And what are my own travels and my age and my death beside this brutal fire in the universe? Tiny, tiny, insignificant. My God, the little that I know of your sun, and this but one among a sea of suns, belittles me. How is it that you love me?

Yet this is but the first of the levels of knowledge of your creation. Of the second level, I am ignorant and left to guess, conjecture only.

For who can say, of those who did not see it, how first you bulged that sun into its place, and hammered its brazen face, and shocked it at the heart and set it afire? Who knows the word wherewith you commanded the sun to be? Who knows the beginning of the things which we *can* know? Theory! Theory! We

chirp theories like chickadees, because ignorance is a terrifying
thing and we need the noise. But when I can with courage know I
do not know; when I admit that I stand with my back to a void,
that I am indeed blind to the beginning of things, then I am silenced. Then I am chilled by my own triviality—some dust at the
edge of a desert. Nevertheless, you kneel down, and find me, and
tell me that you love me.

Yet there is a final level of knowledge from which I am shut
altogether. Of this I cannot even guess. I gape alone, and wonder.

For you who made the sun, the metagalaxies, and the hairs on
the head of my daughter Mary, you first of all created space in
which these things could be. Ah, mighty God! Space, where there
had been no space? Dimension, where none had been before?
Not just the *things* do I now consider, but the room that contains
them. Nor just this room or that, but *room itself.* My Lord, I
haven't the language anymore, not the least imagination of the act
you acted *before* the beginning of things. For someone might
imagine a space in which nothing is; but no one can imagine a
nothing in which not even space is.

Thou Deity, holy, mighty, and immortal!

Panto Krator! From whom the cosmos, on whom the found-
ing of all things, by whom existence!

Ah, my Father, how can you love me so?

For even as you created space in which things are, so also you
created time in which events occur. These two creations, space
and time, are each as elemental as the other.

And even as I am dust in space, so am I but an instant in
time—always an instant, never more than this particular instant:
the end of the year that ended yesterday, the beginning of the
year that begins today, the first day of that year, the morning of
that day, the minute, the second that ticks for me *now.* How insignificant, small, and pipping this moment! How like a rat's tooth,
unworthy of any memory. Yet it is me. And behold! You enter
from the other side of time; you stride from timelessness to this

sole moment, to the ragged stretch of my existence, to me, to love me. How can such a kindness be?

For you who made time are not bound by time—except you choose to be.

You embrace me, my dribble of moments. Right now you are standing at my birth, receiving me an infant into this created world. Yet right now you are present for this prayer of mine, prayed between the years. But right now you are establishing the answers of our prayers in our futures, in your present. And right now, right now, dear God, you are waiting at my death, your hands extended, ready to receive me to your kingdom—not only the same God as hears me now, but in the same eternal moment as now I pray!

Ah, Lord, who, before Abraham was, *is!*

Eternal God, such thoughts are too wonderful for me. They are high: I cannot attain unto them.

For you are wonderful beyond describing it. And yet you love me. And still you choose to notice me. And nonetheless, you bend your boundless being, your infinity, into space and time, into things and into history, to find me, to preserve my life.

Abba, Abba, Father!

How is it that you care for me?

I whisper, amazed that you should care to hear it; I whisper, astonished that it could make a difference to the Deity; I whisper here, now, the truth of my heart and the wholeness of my being:

I whisper, God, I love you, too.

An Advent Monologue

I LOVE A CHILD.

But she is afraid of me.

I want to help this child, so terribly in need of help. For she is hungry; her cheeks are sunken to the bone; but she knows little of food, less of nutrition. I know both these things. She is cold, and she is dirty; she lives at the end of a tattered hallway, three flights up in a tenement whose landlord long forgot the human bodies huddled in that place. But I know how to build a fire; and I know how to wash a face.

She is retarded, if the truth be told, thick in her tongue, slow in her mind, yet aware of her infirmity and embarrassed by it. But here am I, well-traveled throughout the universe, and wise, and willing to share my wisdom.

She is lonely all the day long. She sits in a chair with her back to the door, her knees tucked tight against her breasts, her arms around these, her head down. And I can see how her hair hangs to her ankles; but I cannot see her face. She's hiding. If I could but see her face and kiss it, why I could draw the loneliness out of her.

She sings a sort of song to pass the time, a childish melody, though she is a woman in her body by its shape, a swelling at her belly. She sings, "Puss, puss." I know the truth, that she is singing of no cat at all, but of her face, sadly, calling it ugly. And I know the truth, that she is right. But I am mightily persuasive myself, and I could make it lovely by my love alone.

I love the child.
But she is afraid of me.

———◆———

Then how can I come to her, to feed and to heal her by my love? Knock on the door? Enter the common way?

No. She holds her breath at a gentle tap, pretending that she is not home; she feels unworthy of polite society. And loud, imperious bangings would only send her into shivering tears, for police and bill collectors have troubled her in the past.

And should I break down the door? Or should I show my face at the window? Oh, what terrors I'd cause then. These have happened before. She's suffered the rapings of kindless men, and therefore she hangs her head, and *therefore* she sings, "Puss."

I am none of these, to be sure. But if I came the way that they have come, she would not know me different. She would not receive my love, but might likely die of a failed heart.

I've called from the hall. I've sung her name through cracks in the plaster. But I have a bright trumpet of a voice, and she covers her ears and weeps. She thinks each word an accusation.

I could, of course, ignore the doors and walls and windows, simply appearing before her as I am. I have that capability. But she hasn't the strength to see it and would die. She is, you see, her own deepest hiding place, and fear and death are the truest doors against me.

Then what is left? How can I come to my beloved? Where's the entrance that will not frighten nor kill her? By what door can love arrive after all, truly to nurture her, to take the loneliness away, to make her beautiful, as lovely as my moon at night, my sun come morning?

———◆———

I know what I will do.

I'll make the woman herself my door—and by her body enter in her life.

Ah, I like that. I like that. However could she be afraid of her own flesh, of something lowly underneath her ribs?

I'll be the baby waking in her womb. Hush: she'll have the time, this way, to know my coming first before I come. Hush: time to get ready, to touch her tummy, touching the promise alone, as it were. When she hangs her head, she shall be looking at me, thinking of *me*, loving me while I gather in the deepest place of her being. It is an excellent plan! Hush.

And then, when I come, my voice shall be so dear to her. It shall call the tenderness out of her soul and loveliness into her face. And when I take milk at her breast, she'll sigh and sing another song, a sweet Magnificat, for she shall feel important then, and worthy, seeing that another life depends on hers. My need shall make her rich!

Then what of her loneliness? Gone. Gone in the bond between us, though I shall not have said a word yet. And for my sake she shall wash her face, for she shall have a reason then.

And the sins that she suffered, the hurts at the hands of men, shall be transfigured by my being: I make good come out of evil; I *am* the good come out of evil.

I am her Lord, who loves this woman.

And for a while I'll let her mother me. But then I'll grow. And I will take my trumpet voice again, which once would kill her. And I'll take her, too, into my arms. And out of that little room, that filthy tenement, I'll bear my mother, my child, alive forever.

I love a child.

But she will not fear me for long, now.

Look! Look, it is almost happening. I am doing a new thing—and don't you perceive it? I am coming among you, a baby.

And my name shall be Emmanuel.

To a Lady with Whom I've Been Intimate, Whose Name I Do Not Know

YOU. I SAW YOU in the Great Scot Supermarket tonight, and now I can't sleep on account of you—thinking that, perhaps, you're not sleeping either.

Ah, you! You count your coins with bitten nails, not once but again and again. This is the way you avoid the checker's eyes, as though ashamed of the goods you buy, as though they declare your loneliness at midnight:

Two six-packs of Tab, because your buttocks, sheathed in shorts, are enormous and hump up your back as you shift your weight from foot to foot. You sigh. I think that you do not know how deeply you sigh, nor yet that I am behind you in the line.

Four frozen dinners whose cartons assure you that there is an apple dessert inside. Swiss steak, roast beef in gravy, chicken drumsticks, shrimp. Which one will you save for Sunday dinner? Do you dress up for Sunday dinner? Do you set the table neatly when the dinner thaws? Or do you eat alone, frowning?

Liquid breakfasts, a carton of Marlboros, five Hershey bars, Tampax, vitamins with iron, a *People* magazine, Ayds to fight an appetite, two large bags of potato chips. At the very last minute you toss a Harlequin paperback on the counter. Is this what you read at Sunday dinner? Is this your company?

What private wars are waged between your kitchen and your bathroom? Here I see an arsenal for both sides: the *She* who would lose weight against the *She* who asks, "Why?" and "So what?"—the *She* whose desires are fed too much, even while they're hardly fed at all. "It's your own fault," the first accuses; "two tons were never tons of love." But the other cries, "If I were loved I would not need to eat."

Ah, you.

Rubber thongs on your feet. The polish on your toenails has grown a quarter inch above the cuticle. I notice this because when the checker rings your bill, you drop a quarter which rolls behind me in the line. I stoop to pick it up. When I rise, your hand is already out and you are saying, "Thanks," even before I have returned it to you.

But I do a foolish thing, suddenly, for which I now ask your forgiveness. I didn't know how dreadfully it would complicate your night.

I hold the quarter an instant in my hand; I look you in the eyes—grey eyes of an honest, charcoal emotion—and I say, "Hello." And then I say, "How are you?" I truly meant that question. I'm sorry.

Shock hits your face. For one second you search my eyes; your cheeks slacken, then, as though they lost their restraint and might cry. That frightens me: what will I do if you cry? But then your lips curl inward; your nostrils flare; the grey eyes flash; and all at once you are very, very angry.

Like a snake your left hand strikes my wrist and holds it, while the right scrapes the quarter from my hand. I am astonished, both by your strength and by your passion.

You hissed when you hurt me. I heard it and remember it still. Then you paid, crunched the sacks against your breast, and walked out into the night, the thongs sadly slapping at your heels.

Ah, you. You.

How much I must have hurt you by my question. Was that mild commonplace too much a probe, too lethal, too threatening for the delicate balance your life has created for itself? Does kindness terrify you because then, perhaps, you would have to do more than dream, more than imagine the Harlequin, but then would have to *be*?

I think so.

To cross the gulf from Life Alone to Life Beloved—truly to be real, truly to be worthy in the eyes of another—means that you are no more your own possession. You give yourself away, and then games all come to an end. No longer can you pretend excuses or accusations against the world; nor can you imagine lies concerning your beauty, your gifts and possibilities. Everything becomes what it really is, for you are *seen* and you know it. "How are you" triggers "Who are you." And it wasn't so much that I said it, but rather that I *meant* it and that I awaited an answer, too—this caused the lonely *She* to know her loneliness, even in the moment when I offered you the other thing: friendship.

It's frightening, isn't it?

To be loved, dear lady, you must let all illusions die. And since, between the bathroom and the kitchen, between *People* magazine and the Harlequin, your Self was mostly illusion—at least the acceptable self—then to be loved meant that your very Self had to die—at least the acceptable self.

Instead, you attacked, and my wrist is still bruised tonight. Ah, you.

A rich young ruler came to Jesus, desiring eternal life. He announced that he had kept all the commandments and wondered whether that weren't enough. But Jesus told him he lacked one thing. He ought, said Jesus, to sell all that he had and give the money to the poor. Upon these words, two were made sorrowful: the rich, because he could not lose his riches, which were his

identity and his Self; he turned away. And Jesus, because he loved
and could not love this man, for the man had turned away.

Riches. O my dear and lonely lady, how rich are you in your
illusions. Ironically, you cling to the very loneliness that you despise. It feels safe. But love—God's love—always comes in light.
That's what scares you. Light illumines truth: obesity, the foolish game
between Ayds and potato chips, between cigarettes and vitamins.
These things are the truth. These you hide. Yet it is only truth that
Jesus can love. He cannot love your imaginings, your riches. Sell
all that you have. Undress—

Not me, after all. It is Jesus who asks, "How are you?" And if
you would then sell the false self by which you sustain the con-
temptible Self and die; if you would answer truly, "I'm fat, helpless and alone, unlovely," then he would love you. No: then you
would *know* that he has loved you all along. To see one truth is to
discover the other—which is that he loves you not because you
are lovable, but because he is love. And here is the power of his
love, that it makes ugliness beautiful! To be loved of God is to be
lovely indeed.

All night long I keep a quarter back and ask, "How are you?"
I can't sleep, waiting for the truth: "I'm just terrible." For then I
would cry, "Good! Now there's a confession I can love!"

———◆———

And the mighty God, the trumpet-voiced, cries, "I love a child.
But she is afraid of me. Then how can I come to her, to feed and
to heal her by my love?—"

Epiphanies

Signs! Signs! A singular star
  Outblazing constellations
Inscribed the sky in this regard:
  "A King for all the nations."
The Magi read the word,
  And sought the Lord,
  And found the Lord.

Signs! Signs! A thundering dove
  Descended to creation
Itself a symbol, Sacred Love,
  Its cry a consecration:
  "Beloved Son, with Thee
  Am I well pleased,
  Am I well pleased."

Signs! Signs! Consignments of wine
  Surpassing sixty gallon
Renewed a wedding in decline
  When lesser spirits failed them.
And who had done this? Who?
  Disciples knew.
  Disciples knew.

Signs! Signs! A face was inflamed,
    The noonday sun descending;
Both Moses and Elijah came;
    The cloud cried out, commending
To Peter, James, and John
    "A Son, my Son,
        Beloved One!"

Signs! Signs! The world is a book,
    And what is not the writing?
The world is charged, for those that look,
    With grandeur, God's reminding:
    In all things near to thee
        Oh, read and see
        Divinity!
    Then name these mysteries
        Epiphanies!
        Epiphanies!

Epiphanies:
Little Children Leading

STILL THE LORD, the Lord God, merciful, gracious, long-suffering and good, whispers on the side of his holy mountain: "I love a child. But he is stone in the palm of my hand. Then how shall I make him to know me, how crack his heart with the hammer, forgiveness?—"

———————— ◆ ————————

The water had no right to be wine.

Six jars stood empty; that was demonstrable. Then Jesus issued a command, and the servants heard it, and the servants, prepared by Mary's ministration, obeyed; that sequence, too, was clear, evident, and reasonable. Soon water brimmed in the six jars, and no one wondered at that. Fill a jar, and water will brim in a jar: it was the natural result of servants' obedient labor, and thus far the process was properly consequential, each detail proceeding from a former constellation of details. Cause and effect. This was common and in the order of things.

Jesus issued a second command, and again the servants heard, and again they obeyed. They dipped liquid and served it to the master of ceremonies, and he drank. But he swallowed wine. *That* was not reasonable! The wine had no right to be there. Somewhere a breach had broken the sequence. Some *un*demonstrable cause had cracked the logic; some invisible force had a very visible, manifest effect, and tasty: wine. According to natural processes, the wine had no right to be there.

So something unnatural, something most uncommon was present in that place. The disciples stared at Jesus—deep, deep, deeper than his brow and down the hallways of his eyes. Rabbi, who are you? Water has no right to be wine—except that God be in you.

For the moment the disciples surrendered logic. They accepted that a door had opened in the universe. They took the impossible production as a sign and worked backward to a cause they had not seen, for flesh and spirit abide on different planes, and their eyes were flesh: "We see the light, even if we cannot see the source of light." Light and source together they called the Glory of God—and they believed on him.

Even so did Jesus reveal himself.

Even so he does.

Listen: here is a story historically true.

My son Matthew has always been borderline hyperactive. This is a very exhausting condition for all concerned, and unnerving. The kid leaped before he crawled and played football before he talked. He watched the televised games with his whole body—that is, he ran every play in the living room, dropping back for the quarterback, shooting forward for the wide receiver, making magnificent dives for bullet-balls, and then managing even to tackle himself against glass hutches and expensive china. Matthew was the whole damn team, at the age of four, in a poor man's living room.

Now, I am a patient man. I'm a pastor; I'm paid to be patient. I spent many a Sunday afternoon in painful patience, practicing this virtue, this fruit of the Spirit—and sometimes I would slip, suddenly delivering myself of a stentorian sermon in a living room before one wide-eyed four-year-old, damping his enthusiasm for a while; but I would generally regain my patience again, presenting my son with an admirable example of Christian restraint. *Restraint*, Matthew. Self-control! See? This is how it's done.

Through my teeth: Ssssee? *This* is how it's done.

But Matthew heard other drums. Matthew took other examples, each of them more vigorous than the last, and terrifying to a father's heart.

He watched what he called "the Six Millions Dollar Man" with worshipful attention. But that which he watches he believes in. And that which he believes in he becomes. The completeness of this kid's loyalty is an inspiration to all the faithful anywhere. No better disciple existed. Let him teach the saints of sainthood. But for God's sake, let him believe in the meek—not the Six Millions Dollar Man!

For the Six Millions Dollar Man, having indestructible right extremities, destroyed things.

There came the day when, in order to find some peace for my work, I commanded my son to his bedroom then bowed my head over my typewriter and trembled for a moment in the cool silence. Silence is a blessed thing. And patience is a virtue. I raised my head and began to type a sentence, tentatively. Another sentence followed, and soon a paragraph developed. It was wonderful. I found my stride; I was on the way to a full page, entertaining visions of a possible chapter before the day was through—when an almighty *crash* erupted from Matthew's bedroom. No, it was more like a *bang!* together with splintering wood.

Up on my poor legs, flying to the bedroom, my fingers still crooked to typewriter keys—

The bedroom door was still shut. No matter. I could read instantly what the Six Millions Dollar Boy had done—for his foot stuck *through the door* two and a half feet above the floor. When I opened it in the proper fashion, I dragged a child out, smiling, on his back. "Hi, Dad," he said. "I tried to come out—"

Through my teeth: strangled screams and very heavy judgment upon a child's head. I soon took the smile from his face, even before we took his foot from the door. The flying boy.

———◆———

At the age of eight, Matthew ran away from home.

This is the cause-effect sequence, as best as I can remember it; there is a bleak, reasonable logic to every successive step, and I can understand that he should have run away:

At night we prayed a regular prayer, certain portions of which I italicized for the edification of my son. We prayed, "Jesus Savior, wash away/ all that has been wrong today/ Help me every day to be / *good and gentle*/ more like thee."

And then sons Matthew and Joseph were to close their eyes in a fine and tired obedience and go to sleep.

But on a particular night particular energies sizzled in my Matthew.

I folded my hands, standing between their beds. We were a picture of familial devotion.

"Jesus Savior/wash away/all that has been wrong today/Help us every day—Matthew! What are you doing?"

Dear Matthew had slipped from covers and concentration, was sitting on the floor, emptying a cardboard box of some 3000 football cards. "Sorting my cards," he said. "Terry Bradshaw—" He's a Steelers fan.

"No you're not." Through my teeth. "We're praying. It's time to go to sleep. In bed, please. Fold your hands, please. Now: Jesus Savior, wash away/all that has been wrong today/Help us— *Matthew! What are you doing?*"

He was trotting out of the room. He was going toward the bathroom. "To brush my teeth."

Jesus! Savior! Well, but tooth-brushing is my rule, after all; and the boy is obeying a rule, grant him that. And I shouldn't countermand rules that earlier I had extolled with wonderful proofs of importance. Patience is a virtue. I let him go. I bowed my head and waited. Patience is a virtue, yes; but Vesuvius is a volcano.

When he returned, broad-grinning, white-toothed, content with himself, we made white-knuckled folds of our hands again, and again we drove into our prayer: "Jesus / Savior / Wash / Away! All that has been / wrong—MATTHEW! WHERE ARE YOU GOING?"

To the bathroom. To the bathroom. To pee!

And what was I to do? If he did not go to the bathroom to pee, the kid would pee in his bed, and then his mother and my wife would find good reason to become his protector and my adversary, herself defeated by wet, stinking sheets.

When he bounced back into the bedroom and back into his bed; when he folded his hands so sweetly, he noticed a certain smolder in my countenance.

"Aren't we going to pray?" he said.

"Tomorrow!" I roared. "We wore the prayer out tonight."

"Aren't you going to hug me?" he said.

"Tomorrow!" I thundered, and left.

Tomorrow.

Breakfast.

My wife called the children, four of them, to wash their hands to eat. Three of them washed their hands. One of them didn't budge, was reading the sports page in the living room.

I was no longer a patient man. "Matthew," I said, "didn't you hear your mother?"

"Yes," he said, "I heard her."

"What did she say?"

"She said, 'Wash your hands.'"

"And why haven't you washed your hands?"

In perfect innocence the child looked up at me from the floor. With perfect rationality, lifting two fingers, he answered me: "Because she didn't ask me twice."

All my rhetorical skills, honed these ten years in the pulpit, flashed in the living room, slammed the walls, damned a child for a no-account and withered his soul to nothing. In round and echoing terms I did condemn the boy. In the language of Moses and the prophets, I sinned against my son.

That afternoon he ran away.

Clarence Fields, Cub Scout leader, called from Church. "Isn't Matthew coming today?" he said.

"He should have come straight from school," I said.

"That's an hour ago. He isn't here yet," said Clarence.

I covered the mouthpiece and spoke to Joseph in the kitchen. "Do you know where Matthew is?"

His brother said, "Yes." Then he said, "No."

"What does that mean?" I asked.

Joseph's eyes were wounded and near tears. "He ran away," said Joseph. "But I don't know where he went."

"From home?"

"He said he wasn't worth nothing. He said he wasn't coming back."

Then Joseph cried.

And a hammering began in my own chest. It was no easy thing to tell Clarence that Matthew ran away. This was my son. This was my doing.

The Cub Scouts immediately deployed, all leaping into Mr. Fields' car and good-deeding it through the city at high speeds, crying, "Matthew!" out the windows.

For my own part, I didn't know what to do. There was water in me that threatened to drown my soul—and I could have been glad to die, or to weep, one. Lord, how I have mishandled my son, my son, my busy, exuberant, vulnerable son!

I went out the front door. I wandered into Bayard Park and began to cross it through trees. Oh, my son, what have I done to you?

Guilt is a very real pain, thick in the chest, sharp in the gut, and almost intolerable. The guilty man will hunch and cup his belly in order to hold the pain; but a broken posture does not ease it: there is no one to blame but himself.

Then I saw him—Matthew, dragging his little self across Powell and into the park, coming home.

I didn't touch him. I hadn't the right. I held my distance and fell in step beside him.

"You ran away?" I asked, to be talking, to hear him talk.

"Yes."

"But you came home." I said that as brightly as I could, as though things were made right thereby.

He said, "I saw a man. I thought he was going to kidnap me. I was afraid. So I came home."

Ah, Matthew! The home that I made for you is only the lesser of two fears—a place to hide in, not to live in. Ah, Matthew! Tiny child at my side.

I had no more words to say, a wretched father. We went home in silence, he to his room, I to my study, where I sat in my chair and could not move. I faced the open door and grieved for the past and the future together. Earth stood still.

I think it was a half hour later that Matthew passed that door toward the stereo, glanced in, saw me, and stopped.

"You okay?" he said.

"No," I said.

"Are you sick?"

"No. Yes."

He gazed at me a moment, perplexed, and I dropped my eyes. Without a sound, neither sobbing nor sighing, I cried.

"Oh-h-h," said Matthew softly. "No, Dad," he said, "don't worry." He came into the study and put his hand on my knee. "I love you," he said. He smiled briefly. And he left.

That child! *That child had no right to forgive me so!* Where did he get the knowledge? Where did he get the maturity, the might of an ageless mercy, the transfiguring power to make me *his* son, and to make his son *free?* No, this was not logical. The sequence, somewhere between my sin and his charity, was breached; some other cause had cracked into the process: he was wine! And I—sweetly limp in my chair—whispered, "Except God be in you."

A door had opened in the universe, and through my son, and in my face. The Glory of the Lord had burst from a little child. Not Sunday school lessons, nor all the sermons he had heard me preach, nor the smattering of Bible reading that the child had done, but Jesus Christ himself was the cause of this most dramatic and real wonder. Matthew didn't speak the Christ; for an instant Matthew *was* the Christ—or rather, Christ abode in him, and I saw it; not with my eyes, for that was his own short-fingered hand on my knee, but with my soul, to which the Word had penetrated, changing it. He had done so casually what in fact he could not do. Only God could do that. But I was most certainly done: I was forgiven indeed.

Even so did Jesus reveal himself and sign my soul.

Even so he does.

And I believe on him.

Time and the Christ

The first of the first day's dawn was white,
That detonation of Time, white;
That primal verb and the birth of being,
Fiat! from the yawp of God,
Was a shout of light,
Was a perfect howl of progenitive light—white!
     And in between,
     The whole earth's springing green.

Then this shall be the evening
End of Time's long westering—
When the phenomenal noun dispredicates
And the growl of God has closed debate
And the light descends in separates—
This: universal purple gloom.
     But in between,
     The whole earth's springing green.

And the Christ's intrusion in Time was white,
The re-murmuring of the First Word, white;
So that advent requires a swaddling white.
     But the King's conclusion's imperial,
     For the Judge shall conjugate us all.
     Oh, *that* advent demands a purple pall.

Yet in between—
All in between—
The whole earth's springing green. . . .

Wheat, and the young vine, green;
Shoots, and the small stalk, sweetly green;
And the tree unfolds and flattens high
A gang of hands to weave the sky,
An audience, applauding light—
And green! Ten thousand leaves are busy green!
For the grace of the spacious Time between
Is the whole earth, springing green.
All in between,
The good earth's springing green.

Modern Hexameron:
De Aranea

THE SPIDER'S THE SPINNER, the spinster, the busy web-weaver, often a widow—for embarrassing reasons—and a homemaker generally careless of her children. Most commonly, she swaddles her eggs together with a stunned bit of food against the day of the children's emergence, and then she takes her leave before she has taken their measure, or seen their faces, or named them.

Little of love in most of the spinsters. Personal survival, rather, and a life, though lasting, lonely: suitors and visitors alike fast become corpses. Her dining room's a morgue.

Plainly: she eats them that come to her.

She's very much like the rest of us: she allows a little fly his shape and the illusion of wholeness; but she has drunk his insides, and he is hollow, in fact; has become his own casket, as it were; his own memorial.

It is a neat, deceptive way to eat. But she has no stomach of her own, you see. She can digest nothing within her. Therefore her prey must also *be* her stomach. Through tiny punctures she injects into a bounden fly digestive juices; inside *his* body his organs and nerves and tissues are broken down, dissolved, and turned to warm soup. This soup she swills—

—even as the most of us swill souls of one another after having cooked them in various enzymes: guilt, humiliations, subjectivities, cruel love—there are a number of fine, acidic mixes. And some among us are so skilled with the hypodermic word that our dear ones continue to sit up and to smile, quite as though they were still alive. But the evidence of eating is in our own fatness. Neither we nor the spinster can conceal fatness.

———◆———

But (and this *but* is no ordinary conjunction: it is graceful altogether!) there is one species of spider different from all the others. Not that she has a stomach. She is a spider, after all, with all the external properties of her genus; with them, she lacks a stomach.

No, it is her manner that makes her wonderful. A man might almost weep to see how she *behaves.*

For this one does not leave her eggs to chance.

She stays. She protects the eggs in incubation. By the hundreds she gathers her brood upon her back so that she seems a grotesque sort of lump, rumpled and swollen. But such is love: it makes the lover ugly.

And when the children emerge, she feeds them. Her juices soften the meat to their diminutive snorkels. Yet even this care, peculiar among the spinsters, does not give her a name above all other names. Many mothers mother their children; that is not uncommon. Rather, it is the last supper which she reserves against necessity that astonishes the watcher and makes him wonder to see heaven in a tiny thing. . . .

Sometimes food grows scarce, and no amount of netting can snare the fly that isn't there. Sometimes tiny famine descends upon the mother and her spiderlings, and then they starve, and then they may die, if they do not eat.

But then, privately, she performs the deed unique among the living.

Into her own body this spinster releases the juices that digest. Freely they run through her abdomen while she holds so still, digesting not some other meat, but her own, breaking down the parts of her that kept her once alive, until her eyes are flat.

She dies.

She becomes the stomach for her children, and she herself the food.

And Jesus said to those who stood around him, "I am the bread of life. I am the living bread which came down from heaven; if any one eats of this bread, he will live forever; and the bread which I will give for the life of the world is my flesh."

Take—and eat.

This one was different from all the rest of us: cooked on a cross.

My Lord! My Lord, how can this be? All the world did shiver and teach me to despise the spider. Yet it was in her that I heard your voice.

The Cry of the Whole Congregation

THE FOLLOWING DRAMA TAKES place on the Sunday of the Passion. Its purpose is to allow each worshiper suddenly to discover (pitifully, intensely, truly to discover) his own rootedness in the drama that is Christ's—so that the Passion Story may no longer be mere story for observance, analysis, learning, or history; so that it embrace the worshiper, name him, and become his own story indeed: the shape of his being.

Therefore, all senses are enlisted: sight, sound, the rhythm of both—music and motion—and the feel of the worshiper's voice in his throat and his emotion in his breast. This drama has no audience. All are actors. None objective. All subjective—or else the objects *of* the driving love of God.

There are four readers:

1. The Narrator, responsible both for narrative material and for the words of Jesus.

2. The Judas figure, who also represents the unrepentant criminal.

3. The Peter figure, who also represents that criminal who repents and receives the promise of the Lord—thus, forgiveness follows sin.

4. The Pilate figure, who also reads the Pharisee's lines during the entrance into Jerusalem and later represents Joseph of Arimathea—by which device, again, forgiveness is signaled.

The congregation as a whole shifts its identity so that it suffers the common conversion of the Christian, which is often an extended, dramatic process: that is, it begins with the ignorant praise of the multitude who knew not what sort of Messiah this Jesus was; next, it is the disciples, loving but failing the Lord; next, it plays the neutral role of the watchers, the questioners who disturb Peter by their curiosity; next, it descends to the sinful shrieks of manipulated people crying, "Crucify." This is the congregation's deepest level. Next, it arises to play out an internal conflict: men and women divide in their speaking, and some lament the deed, praying forgiveness, while others clearly participate in the deed. In "Crucify" they sinned; in this passage, though they continue in sin, yet they are conscious of it, too; and that is the more painful state, to be sure, but it is also the better, being the beginning of confession. Next, with the repentant criminal, the congregation recognizes the kingdom, power, glory of the Lord; and finally it is the women, blessedly separated from the event, yet witnesses unto it. Witnesses!

In the congregation's shifting role, the Lord's Prayer plays a constant harmony to the Lord's passion, again and again thrusting the people (by their connotative memory of these significant words) into a worshipful attitude—making real not only to the mouth and the mind but also to the soul what is taking place today.

There is a dancer. She is female. She alone takes the chancel, in which no furniture is but the rail and the altar. Nor does she enter the rail and approach the altar until that moment when Jesus is crucified—and then her feet are rooted and motion appears in her upper body only. At death her head and body sag. At burial she crumples altogether. Before then she may use the passages of music—particularly when the congregation sings—for sweeping steps and speed. But she will also vary her presentation so that sometimes it closes in on mime; for example, during the words of the Last Supper, "This is my body," she will seem to draw from her very abdomen the invisible gift which then she proffers; and at the right moments she will turn her head through sad degrees to look at Judas, to gaze upon the Peter figure.

The congregation, as it busies itself in reading and singing, shall catch fleeting images of this dancer—and so shall she effect a metaphorical communication. Since they shall not see her whole and lineal, they will find themselves unconsciously filling in the blanks; and what they give to her by imagination shall be diverse among them and mighty indeed.

Please note that she does not play Christ. Rather, she represents, as best as possible, the moods, the changes he must have passed through. She represents both his suffering and his love.

There is a drummer. He teaches the congregation its rhythm, beginning very slowly and softly, but increasing speed and impact as the drama unfolds, nipping the people's heels like a sheepdog, driving them, making them restless and thumping thunder to their cries of "Crucify! Crucify!" In the last passages of the cross, just before Jesus dies, his beat becomes the death march, funereal and impossibly sad. At death he falls silent altogether—and that silence shall be *heard*. It shall be deep space and a dangerous thing. I promise you: at that moment not a member of the congregation shall move, for death will be very present against their hearts.

There is a soloist—a male and tenor, if possible. He may be accompanied on piano for the first three verses of his piece. But the last verse must be sung a cappella, for it must be very lonely. For the first three verses—as for the passages which the congregation sings—the drummer and the dancer fall in rhythm.

There is a children's choir. They, together with all the other principals, process during the first hymn and take positions ready to sing; their still presence there will draw the attention of the congregation and its anticipation. But when their piece is finished, they take their seats. They should be versed in reading the congregational role, for they will lend dear credulity to the sound;

moreover, the children ought *never* to be forgotten! They know better than we how to hear a story and how to discover the value of it. The theology shall escape them; but the drama shall catch them up. And isn't that the better thing anyway? Isn't theology simply the drama's interpretation?

Finally, this drama, as written, is essentially Lucan. But the author has sometimes been free with the text.

Oh, and this is not considered extracurricular. This is worship indeed.

WORSHIP FOR THE WAY OF THE CROSS

1. *The Entry into Jerusalem*

(Four readers' stands are visible before the chancel and empty. All is emptiness. A gentle flurry on the drum draws the congregation's attention, out of which rhythm a slow two-note fanfare of the organ rises and lowers again. Before it is silenced, while yet it holds last notes long, long, the narrator begins to read from the back of the church. His voice is clear and declarative.)

NARRATOR: When Jesus drew near to Bethphage and Bethany, at the mount that is called Olivet, he sent ahead two of his disciples, saying, "Go into the village opposite. There you will find a colt tied, on which no one has ever yet sat; untie it and bring it here. If any one asks you, 'Why are you untying it?' you shall say, 'The Lord has need of it.' "

(During the next portion of the narrator's reading, let the Peter and the Judas figures walk forward to their stands.)

NARRATOR: So those who were sent went away and found it as he had told them. . . .

PEOPLE: AND AS THEY WERE UNTYING THE COLT, ITS OWNERS SAID TO THEM, "WHY ARE YOU UNTYING THE COLT?"

PETER: And they said, "The Lord has need of it." And they brought it to Jesus, and throwing their garments on the colt, they set Jesus upon it.

(*As the narrator reads the next portion, the organist plays once through the music of the coming hymn, swelling so that the narrator must raise his voice louder and louder.*)

NARRATOR: (*Processing slowly, the whole company of presenters and the children's choir following with good space between each.*) And as he rode along, they spread their garments on the road. As he was now drawing near, at the descent of the Mount of Olives, the whole multitude of the disciples began to rejoice and to praise God with a loud voice for all the mighty works that they had seen, saying:

PEOPLE: (*Singing this or another hymn of high praise, preferably one with messianic titles, certainly one they know well; an excellent choice would be the traditional Sanctus, if the people know it and can be lusty about it. Then it would be sung through twice, the organist pedaling down between verses—as here—for the shouted exchange between the Pharisee and Jesus.*)

Refrain:
ALL GLORY, LAUD AND HONOR TO THEE REDEEMER
  KING,
TO WHOM THE LIPS OF CHILDREN MADE SWEET
  HOSANNAS RING.
THOU ART THE KING OF ISRAEL, THOU DAVID'S ROYAL
  SON,
WHO IN THE LORD'S NAME COMEST, THE KING AND
  BLESSED ONE.
Refrain.
THE COMPANY OF ANGELS ARE PRAISING THEE ON HIGH,
CREATION AND ALL MORTALS IN CHORUS MAKE REPLY.
Refrain.
THE MULTITUDE OF PILGRIMS WITH PALMS BEFORE YOU
  WENT;

OUR PRAISE AND PRAYER AND ANTHEMS BEFORE THEE
WE PRESENT.

PHARISEE: *(Shouting.)* And some of the Pharisees in the multitude cried to him, "Teacher, rebuke your disciples! They're calling you the Christ. Tell them to shut up!"

NARRATOR: *(In strong voice over the organ.)* He answered, "I tell you, if these were silent the very stones themselves would cry out."

PEOPLE: *(Singing with the swell of the organ.)*

Refrain—and then:
TO THEE BEFORE THY PASSION THEY SANG THEIR
HYMNS OF PRAISE;
TO THEE WE TOO REPEAT THEM AND MELODIES WE
RAISE.
Refrain.
THOU DIDST ACCEPT THEIR PRAISES; ACCEPT THE
PRAYERS WE BRING,
WHO IN ALL GOOD DELIGHTEST, THOU GOOD AND
GRACIOUS KING.

(All now are in position, the children facing the congregation and prepared to sing.)

NARRATOR: And when he drew near and saw the city he wept over it, saying, "Would that even today you knew the things that make for peace! But now they are hid from your eyes. O Jerusalem! The days shall come upon you, when your enemies will cast up a bank about you and surround you, and hem you in on every side, and dash you to the ground, you and your children within you, and they will not leave one stone upon another in you; because you did not know the time of your visitation."

(Piano introduction to the children's piece begins before the narrator is through, timing it so that there is but a beat or two and the children sing.)

CHILDREN: O Jerusalem, you missed your time to sing,
You missed your loving king
When he came to bring
You healing in his name
And wholeness to the lame;
You were blinded to his reign,
So the children sang:
Hosanna to the Son of David! Hosanna! Hosanna!
    Hosanna!
Hosanna to the Son of David! Hosanna! Hosanna!
    Hosanna,
To the King, to the King, to the King, to the King.*

(This song begins wistfully, rises to joy, ought to be sung at a quick pace, but delivers its last phrases sadly once again. If the children can, they might go to their seats while singing the final phrases; it will give the effect of a dying echo and loneliness.)

2. The Preparation and the Eating of the Last Supper

NARRATOR: Now, the feast of Unleavened Bread drew near, which is called the Passover. And the Temple Priests were seeking how to put Jesus to death; for they feared the people.

JUDAS: Then Satan entered into Judas called Iscariot, who was of the number of the Twelve; he went away and conferred with the temple priests and officers how he might betray him to them. And they were glad, and engaged to give him money. So he agreed, and sought an opportunity to betray him to them in the absence of the multitude.

NARRATOR: Then came the day of Unleavened Bread, on

* "Hosanna to the Son of David" from *Kids of the Kingdom*, words and music by Anne Herring. © 1979 Latter Rain Music. All rights reserved. Used by permission.

which the Passover lamb had to be sacrificed. So Jesus sent Peter and John, saying, "Go and prepare the Passover for us, that we may eat it."

PEOPLE: THEY SAID TO HIM, "BUT WHERE, LORD? WHERE WILL YOU HAVE US PREPARE IT, AND WHAT ARE WE TO DO?"

NARRATOR: He said to them, "Behold, when you have entered the city, a man carrying a jar of water will meet you; follow him into the house which he enters, and tell the householder, 'The Teacher says to you, Where is the guest room, where I am to eat the Passover with my disciples?' And he will show you a large upper room furnished; there make ready." And they went and found it as he had told them; and they prepared the Passover.

(The dancer enters the chancel simply: Jesus at the Last Supper. Quietly, the organist plays "Let Us Break Bread Together on Our Knees" until the narrator has read through the institution of Holy Communion, falling silent immediately before the words, "But behold the hand of him who betrays—" The dancer serves slowly and with clean simplicity.)

NARRATOR: And when the hour came, he sat at table, and the apostles with him. And he said to them, "I have earnestly desired to eat this Passover with you before I suffer. *(Dancer signifies awareness of the congregation:* with you!) For I tell you, I shall not eat it until it is fulfilled in the kingdom of God." And he took the cup, and when he had given thanks he said, "Take this and divide it among yourselves; for I tell you that from now on I shall not drink of the fruit of the vine until the kingdom of God comes." And he took bread *(the dancer draws this from her abdomen)* and when he had given thanks he broke it and gave it to them, saying, "This is my body which is given for you. Do this in remembrance of me." And likewise the cup after supper, saying, "This cup which is poured out for you is the new covenant in my blood. *(Dancer: round with slow fire.)* But behold the hand of him who betrays me is with me on the table. For the Son of Man goes as it has been determined: but woe to that man by whom he is betrayed!"

PEOPLE: AND THEY BEGAN TO QUESTION, "WHO, LORD? WHO IS TO BETRAY YOU? IS IT I? IS IT I?"

NARRATOR: He answered, "He who has dipped his hand in the dish with me will betray me. Oh, it would have been better for that man if he had not been born."

JUDAS: Judas, who betrayed him, said, "Is it I, Master?"

NARRATOR: Jesus said to him, "You have said so."

(Silence a moment while the Judas figure withdraws from his stand and walks to the back of the church.)

PETER: *(With lunging impetuosity, even before Judas is fully gone.)* Simon Peter was indignant. "But not I!" he said. And he declared, "Though they all fall away from you, I will never leave you."

NARRATOR: "Peter, truly I say to you, this very night, before the cock crows, you will deny me three times."

PETER: Peter said to him, "Even if I must die with you, I will never deny you!"

PEOPLE: AND SO SAID ALL OF THE DISCIPLES, OVER AND OVER AGAIN.

(Let these exchanges follow with a tense speed.)

3. The Agony in the Garden

PEOPLE: *(Singing, after the organist has played through the melody once, simply. Let the dancer's motion show the journey and then sorrow.)*

GO TO DARK GETHSEMANE, YE THAT FEEL THE
   TEMPTER'S POWER;
YOUR REDEEMER'S CONFLICTS SEE, WATCH WITH HIM
   ONE BITTER HOUR;
TURN NOT FROM HIS GRIEFS AWAY:
LEARN OF JESUS CHRIST TO PRAY.

NARRATOR: And he came out and went, as was his custom,

to the Mount of Olives; and the disciples followed him. And when he came to the place he said to them, "Pray that you may not enter into temptation."

PEOPLE: LEAD US NOT INTO TEMPTATION, BUT DELIVER US, DELIVER US.

NARRATOR: And he withdrew from them about a stone's throw, and knelt down and prayed, "Father, if thou art willing, remove this cup from me; nevertheless, not my will, but thine be done."

PEOPLE: OUR FATHER WHO ART IN HEAVEN, HALLOWED BE THY NAME. THY KINGDOM COME; THY WILL BE DONE. THY WILL BE DONE. THY WILL BE DONE—

NARRATOR: And when he rose from prayer, he came to the disciples and found them sleeping for sorrow, and he said to them, "Why do you sleep? Rise and pray that you may not enter into temptation."

PEOPLE: LEAD US NOT INTO TEMPTATION, BUT DELIVER US FROM EVIL, EVEN THE EVIL WITHIN OURSELVES.

JUDAS: (*While coming from the back of the church; the dancer signifies awareness of his approach and reacts to him from her distance, especially during the words of the Lord—but none of the readers attempt interaction with the dancer; she's in her world alone, using readers and people as foci.*) While he was still speaking, there came a crowd, and the man called Judas, one of the Twelve, was leading them. He drew near to Jesus to kiss him (*this facing the congregation*),

NARRATOR: But Jesus said to him, "Judas, would you betray the Son of Man with a kiss?"

JUDAS: Judas said, "Hail, Master."

PEOPLE: WHEN THE DISCIPLES SAW WHAT WOULD FOL-LOW, THEY SAID, "LORD, SHALL WE STRIKE WITH THE SWORD?"

PETER: And one of them struck the slave of the high priest and cut off his right ear.

NARRATOR: But Jesus said, "No more of this!" And he touched his ear and healed him.

PEOPLE: FORGIVE US OUR TRESPASSES AS WE FORGIVE THOSE WHO TRESPASS AGAINST US.

NARRATOR: Jesus said to those who had come out against him, "When I was with you day after day in the temple, you did not lay hands on me. But this is your hour, and the power of darkness." (*The organist should begin, during this passage, the music to indicate the next hymn verse, so that the congregation begins to sing immediately after the narrator's next words.*) Then they seized him—

4. The Judgment

PEOPLE:

FOLLOW TO THE JUDGMENT HALL, VIEW THE LORD OF
    LIFE ARRAIGNED;
OH, THE WORMWOOD AND THE GALL! OH THE PANGS
    HIS SOUL SUSTAINED!
SHUN NOT SUFFERING, SHAME OR LOSS;
LEARN FROM HIM TO BEAR THE CROSS.

NARRATOR: Then they seized him and led him away, bringing him to the high priest's house.

PETER: Peter followed at a distance; and when they had kindled a fire in the middle of the courtyard and sat down together, Peter sat among them.

PEOPLE: THEN A MAID, SEEING HIM SIT IN THE LIGHT, SAID, "THIS MAN ALSO WAS WITH HIM."

PETER: But he denied it, saying, "Woman, I do not know him."

PEOPLE: AND A LITTLE LATER SOMEONE ELSE SAW HIM AND SAID, "YOU ALSO ARE ONE OF THEM."

PETER: But Peter said, "Man, I am not."

PEOPLE: AN HOUR LATER ANOTHER INSISTED, SAYING, "CERTAINLY THIS MAN ALSO WAS WITH HIM; FOR HE IS A GALILEAN."

PETER: But Peter said, "Man, I do not know what you are saying!"

NARRATOR: And immediately, while he was still speaking, the cock crowed. And the Lord turned and looked at Peter. (*Let the dancer turn!*)

PETER: And Peter remembered the word of the Lord, how he had said to him, "Before the cock crows today, you will deny me three times." And he went out and he wept bitterly.

(*Silence for Peter—while he walks to the back of the church, precisely as Judas did before him!*)

NARRATOR: Now the men who were holding Jesus mocked him and beat him; they blindfolded him and demanded:

PEOPLE: "PROPHESY! WHO IS IT THAT STRUCK YOU?"

NARRATOR: And they spoke many other words against him, reviling him. (*Pause, head down; continue in subdued yet audible voice, with peace facing the congregation: there should be contrast between Jesus' presentation and the accusers', and contrast between this short scene and the driving one to come. The rhythm is all of a piece, now, till Pilate releases him to the enemies.*) When the day came, the assembly of the elders of the people gathered together and led him to their council;

PEOPLE: AND THEY SAID, "IF YOU ARE THE CHRIST, TELL US."

NARRATOR: But he said to them, "If I tell you, you will not believe; and if I ask you now, you will not answer. But from now on the Son of man shall be seated at the right hand of the power of God—"

PEOPLE: AND THEY SAID, "ARE YOU THE SON OF GOD, THEN?"

NARRATOR: And he said to them, "You say that I am."

PEOPLE: AND THEY SAID, "BLASPHEMY! WHAT FURTHER TESTIMONY DO WE NEED? WE HAVE HEARD IT OURSELVES FROM HIS OWN LIPS. BLASPHEMY! OH, BLASPHEMY!"

(*Boom! One hard knock on the drum signals its presence; a good space of time before the second beat, much softer, and then the third, immediately after which the narrator begins the next scene, the drum's rhythm established.*

It will continue, now, at first far away, but coming louder, faster, nearer as the scene continues, until it beats a dreadful climax on the first syllable of the two words, "Crucify! Crucify!" Let the rhythm be simple—beat, beat, beat—and continual.)

5. Dawn Friday: Jesus Before Pilate

NARRATOR: Then the whole company of them arose, and brought him before Pontius Pilate.

PEOPLE: AND THEY BEGAN TO CURSE HIM, SAYING, "WE FOUND THIS MAN PERVERTING OUR NATION, AND FORBIDDING US TO GIVE TRIBUTE TO CAESAR, AND SAYING THAT HE HIMSELF IS CHRIST THE KING!"

PILATE: And Pilate asked him, "Are you the King of the Jews?"

NARRATOR: And he answered him, "You have said so."

PILATE: And Pilate said to the Chief Priests and the multitudes, "I find no crime in this man."

PEOPLE: BUT THEY WERE URGENT, SAYING, "HE STIRS UP THE PEOPLE, TEACHING THROUGHOUT GALILEE EVEN TO THIS PLACE."

PILATE: And when Pilate heard that he was a Galilean, of Herod's jurisdiction, he sent him to Herod,

NARRATOR: Where he was vehemently accused, and treated with contempt and mocked, and arrayed in gorgeous purple, and then sent back again.

PILATE: Pilate said to the rulers of the people, "You brought me this man as one who was perverting the people; and after examining him, behold, I did not find him guilty of any of the charges against him. Behold, *nothing* deserving death has been done by him. I will therefore chastise him and release him—"

PEOPLE: BUT THEY ALL CRIED OUT TOGETHER, "AWAY WITH THIS MAN! AWAY! AWAY! RELEASE TO US BARABBAS—"

NARRATOR: Barabbas!—a man who had been thrown into prison for insurrection and for murder—

PILATE: Pilate addressed them once more, desiring to release Jesus—

PEOPLE: BUT THEY SHOUTED OUT, "CRUCIFY HIM! CRUCIFY HIM!"

PILATE: "Why? What evil has he done? I've found no crime in him deserving death. I'll chastise him. I'll release him—"

PEOPLE: BUT THEY WERE URGENT, DEMANDING WITH LOUD CRIES THAT HE SHOULD BE CRUCIFIED.

NARRATOR: And their voices prevailed.

PILATE: So Pilate gave sentence that their demand should be granted. He released the man who had been jailed for murder. But Jesus he delivered up to their will.

6. *Friday Morning: Crucifixion*

(The organist plays the melody of the following hymn through once with a single, keening note—a reed?—and makes the people's singing subdued.

The drummer has tempered his passion for a while, playing with rather than against the people's voice rhythm and inclination, and so shall he echo them through the first part of this scene, sadly scoring the soloist's words for two verses. But when the exchange begins between women and men at the foot of the cross, he must teach them the tension of that, the pain of the conflict between sinning and seeking forgiveness; therefore, for the first time he breaks his single-beating rhythm and creates a frenetic one, that their words be pitched back and forth with harder and quicker impact: they find themselves stepping on each others' verbal toes, and distressed.

The dancer, with the processional to the cross and the crucifixion itself, enters the rail for the first time and then faces the congregation, standing immediately before the altar, arms extended, yet motion in the upper body, thus showing both the severe restriction upon our Lord and the pain. But do not overdramatize this agony! Head and shoulders may roll; yet half an action doubles its force; the whole of an action, a mimicked depiction, halves it!)

PEOPLE: CALVARY'S MOURNFUL MOUNTAIN CLIMB. THERE ADORING AT HIS FEET, MARK THAT MIRACLE OF TIME, GOD'S OWN SACRIFICE COMPLETE. "IT IS FINISHED!" HEAR HIM CRY. LEARN FROM JESUS CHRIST TO DIE.

NARRATOR: But Jesus he delivered over to their will.

ALL MEN: AND AS THEY LED HIM AWAY, THEY SEIZED ONE SIMON OF CYRENE, WHO WAS COMING IN FROM THE COUNTRY, AND LAID ON HIM THE CROSS, TO CARRY IT BEHIND JESUS.

ALL WOMEN: AND THERE FOLLOWED HIM A GREAT MULTITUDE OF WOMEN WHO BEWAILED AND LAMENTED HIM—

(The contrast of men- to women-voices will strike a sudden, new dimension: us, but us at odds with ourselves.)

NARRATOR: But Jesus turning to them said, "Daughters of Jerusalem, do not weep for me, but weep for yourselves and for your children. For behold, the days are coming when they will say, 'Blessed are the barren, and the wombs that never bore, and the breasts that never gave suck!' For if they do this when the wood is green, what will happen when it dries!"

SOLO: *(A pause; the piano lightly plays an introduction; the soloist sings with infinite gentleness, and sings this particular piece not only for its familiarity, but also to stress You are there, now!)* Were you there when they crucified my Lord? Oh, sometimes it causes me to tremble, tremble— Were you there when they crucified my Lord?—

(The accompanist plays quietly the chorus while the narrator reads the next passage, so that words and music, the crucifixion, all comes as one single event, unbroken.)

NARRATOR: Two others also, who were criminals, were led away to be put to death with him. *(At this point the Peter figure returns up the aisle of the church, quietly.)* And when they came to the place which is called the Skull, there they crucified him, and the criminals, one on the right and one on the left.

SOLO: *(Immediately.)* Were you there when they nailed him to the tree? Oh, sometimes it causes me to tremble, tremble—Were you there when they nailed him to the tree?

(Drummer: the new rhythm. Establish it under these next words.)

NARRATOR: And Jesus said, "Father, forgive them; for they know not what they do."

ALL WOMEN: FORGIVE US OUR TRESPASSES.

ALL MEN: AND THEY CAST LOTS TO DIVIDE HIS GARMENTS.

ALL WOMEN: FORGIVE US OUR TRESPASSES.

ALL MEN: AND THE PEOPLE STOOD BY, WATCHING. BUT THE RULERS SCOFFED AT HIM, SAYING, "HE SAVED OTHERS; LET HIM SAVE HIMSELF, IF HE IS THE CHRIST OF GOD!"

ALL WOMEN: FORGIVE US OUR TRESPASSES.

ALL MEN: THE SOLDIERS ALSO MOCKED HIM, COMING UP AND OFFERING HIM VINEGAR.

ALL WOMEN: THERE WAS AN INSCRIPTION OVER HIM: "THIS IS THE KING OF THE JEWS."

ALL MEN: FORGIVE US OUR TRESPASSES. FORGIVE US, O LORD, OUR TRESPASSES!

JUDAS: One of the criminals who were hanged with him railed at him, saying, "Are you not the Christ? Save yourself and us!"

PETER: But the other rebuked him, saying, "Do you not fear God, since you are under the same sentence, and we justly? But this man has done nothing wrong." And he said, "Jesus, remember me when you come into your kingdom."

PEOPLE: FORGIVE US OUR TRESPASSES. DELIVER US FROM EVIL. THINE IS THE KINGDOM—

NARRATOR: And Jesus said to him—

PEOPLE: AND THE POWER—

NARRATOR: "Truly, truly, I say to you—"

PEOPLE: AND THE GLORY—

NARRATOR: "Today you will be with me in Paradise."

PEOPLE: FOREVER AND EVER. AMEN!

SOLO: *(Immediately, the intro having been played over previous words):* Were you there when he cried out at the end? Oh, sometimes it causes me to tremble, tremble—Were you there when he cried out at the end?

(Drummer: during that verse you almost disappeared. Now you return with rapidly increasing force, beating a death march, louder and louder and louder until the word "spirit" at which you bang your last tormented bang and be still.)

(Narrator: read this passage with grave pauses, but lift your voice more and more until, when Jesus cries with loud voice, you are roaring at the top of your lungs, but slowly; do not look at the congregation; look at your script. On "Spirit" you, too, shut up totally, tomb-like, and allow the silence to be a shocking, lasting thing. Then speak the death words quietly, as though the thing hath truly just occurred. Again, pause before you give words back to the people. This is a grievous moment; they need the time to grieve.)

NARRATOR: It was now about the sixth hour—and there was darkness over the whole land until the ninth hour, while the sun's light failed. . . . And the curtain of the temple was torn in two, from the top to the bottom. . . . Then Jesus, crying with a loud voice, said, "Father, into thy hands I commend my spirit!" *(Silence. Damnable, deafening silence.)*

And having said this, he breathed his last.

(Pause. The dancer loses the taut position of the last cry, sags gently to death.)

And all the multitudes who had assembled to see the sight,

PEOPLE: WHEN THEY SAW WHAT HAD TAKEN PLACE, RETURNED HOME BEATING THEIR BREASTS.

ALL WOMEN: AND ALL HIS ACQUAINTANCES AND THE WOMEN WHO HAD FOLLOWED HIM FROM GALILEE STOOD AT A DISTANCE AND SAW THESE THINGS—

7. Late Friday Afternoon: Burial

SOLO: *(No piano—the naked voice alone: a cappella, lonely)* Were you there when they laid him in the tomb? Oh, sometimes it causes

me to tremble, tremble—Were you there when they laid him in
the tomb?

PILATE: Now there was a man named Joseph from the town of
Arimathea, a good man, a righteous man, one looking for the kingdom of God. This man went to Pilate and asked for the body of
Jesus. Then he took it down and wrapped it in a linen shroud, and
laid him in a rock-hewn tomb, where no one had ever yet been laid.

NARRATOR: It was the day of Preparation, and the Sabbath
was beginning.

ALL WOMEN: THE WOMEN WHO HAD COME WITH HIM
FROM GALILEE FOLLOWED, AND SAW THE TOMB AND HOW
HIS BODY WAS LAID. THEN THEY RETURNED, AND PREPARED
SPICES AND OINTMENTS—

NARRATOR: On the Sabbath they rested according to the
commandment.

(*Silence. Sit. And done.*)

An excellent hymn with which to conclude this piece is
"Rock of Ages," since it both takes and transfigures the imagery
of this story, making it cleansing and finding the Good News in
this Bad Event. A parish might reverently prepare for Holy Communion at this point, the organist using "Let Us Break Bread Together"; but little else should be required of the people. They will
want to be still with their grieving.

Lily

THREE SISTERS LIVED ON the edge of a wood, an older, a middle, and a younger. They caught the summer sunlight all day long, since their dwelling was on the south side of that wood; and each did something different with the day and the light.

Few took notice when the eldest was born. She had been a plain sort, a simple, skinny sprout growing at a busy pace. But she'd been born with a will, and she said "I'll *make* them notice me!" So she tied up her hair and went to work. She produced a flower that looked like a purse, pale and small and forgettable, and no one noticed, and she said, "Just wait. They'll notice me." She went to work. She made ten of these flowers and more, twenty, fifty, a hundred and more, and she hung them like socks in the sunlight, and still no one noticed, but she said, "You'll see. They'll notice me." Each of her flowers filled up with the sunlight, and then this was the stuff that she worked with. All day long she ground the sunlight, as though it were meat, and she kneaded and squeezed it and pushed and she patted until her stem and her pedicels ached. Water she added and sugars and vitamins, valuable ingredients, basically healthy, though nothing so tasty as spice: this sister knew nothing of spice or excitement. Of the sunlight, then, and of an uncommon amount of work, she produced a food, long like a sausage, moisty green and crisp if you ate it now, nutty and hard and wholesome if you waited till later.

This sister's name was Bean Plant. Soon everyone noticed her. Several hundred members of the Family Fowl made her acquaintance and praised her labor by eating it. And Squirrels, who ate the nut sitting up, gnawing politely and silently, took dinner with her. And before that the Host of Rabbits had praised her salad. Everyone noticed her. Of sunlight and labor she fed a thousand stomachs.

And so it was that she could draw herself up very high and say, "See? I'm a very important person. How could all of these do without me? They couldn't at all, at all. They need me."

The middle sister, on the other hand, produced nothing. She had no desire to weave or whittle, to cook or sew, to hammer or dig or work at a thing. "I," she said, "am important just as I am." And she smiled exquisite smiles on all around her, and all said, "To be sure!"

For when Marigold was born, *everyone* took notice. She was simply beautiful. And when she grew, her blossoms burst forth *like* the sunlight itself, golden-yellow, full and glowing, beatific altogether. The Grandmother Elms said, "Oh." The Willows, her aunts, and all of them spinsters, wept to see such brightness in the world. A hundred suitors stood behind her, tall and handsome, dark and green, named Spruce; and when she danced with the Wind and whirled in his rhythm and trembled to his breath, the Spruce, to a man, made moans because she wasn't dancing with them. And what did she do with the sunlight? Why, she stood in it, was all. She let it shine on her, to everyone's gratification. Happy the souls who saw her, she thought; happy the sun to touch her; and happiest *she* to receive such attentions.

But wasn't she grander than the sun after all? "Of course," she sighed, patting her hair. "I am a knockout. What would the world do without me?"

Bean Plant and Marigold would sometimes discuss their sister. Nor did they lower their voices when they did. They talked about her as though she weren't there, for she was a fool, they thought, and somewhat dim in her brains and helpless, and how could she mind?

"What of Lily?" they said, and they shook their heads.

"What of Lily, indeed." Lily, the youngest of the three.

The child had nothing whatever to recommend her, neither beauty nor skill. She was fat, flat, and green, her tongue stiff and thick; she could not dance to the wind nor produce a single kernel of food; she looked like a walking-stick stuck in the ground and forgotten, no reason to be there, no reason at all. Why, even *she* said, "What of Lily?" when they had said it; for she had searched through her whole being herself and had found nothing of worth.

But what bothered her sisters the most was her habit of talking to the sun. The child was addled, dreamy, and deluded; and who was to say how poorly that might reflect upon two sisters so up in the world? They had their reputations to consider.

"The sun is good for food," Bean Plant told her, "but the sun can't talk."

"Maybe not, and maybe so," said Lily, exasperating the busy sister.

"The sun is good for radiance," Marigold told her, "but the sun can't talk."

"Maybe not, and maybe so," said Lily, irritating the beautiful sister.

But it seemed to Lily that the sun *did* talk. Oh, not in words that anyone could hear, actually. But what he *did* was his talking. To rise in the morning and to peep at her from the greening east and to warm her to the root was his way of saying, "Good," and she said, "Morning," and together, then, they said, "Good morning." And when he did not pause one second in the sky, but crossed it slowly, certainly, surely in such a way as might be trusted absolutely, it seemed to her that he was saying, "Good," and she said, "Day," and together they said, "Good day." And when he laid him down in a purple, westerly bed and grew very big just before he shut out the light, as though he were stretching and yawning, that was how he said, "Good"; and then she never, never said, "Bye," for she would be sad if he went away forever. No, she said, "Night," and so they said, "Good night" together.

This is what Lily did with the sun: she had conversations with him. And always his word was, "Behold, it is very good"; and always her word said *what* was very good—and that was something, since her sisters' words were, "Useless and ugly, idle and plain, and worthless altogether." But Lily never stopped listening to him however they scorned her, because she thought that one day he might say to her, "I love you," which would be a very important thing not to miss, since she knew in her soul that she was a very *un*important person, but loving might make a difference.

"The sun is not a somebody," said Bean Plant and Marigold.

And Lily said, "Maybe not, and maybe so."

And her sisters said, "Ugh! You are impossible."

And Lily said, "That's true."

Then it came to pass that a sadness settled on Lily, and that was further aggravation to her sisters. Lily stupid was one thing. Lily sad was another and noxious altogether.

Dew, it seemed, on the poor child's leaf, dewdrops at the tip end of her spears. These were her tears.

"Be busy," said Bean Plant, "and you'll have no time for moping."

"A fine how-do-you-do," said Marigold. "By bright smiles I can make all the world happy—except my sister, except my own small sister. How do you think that looks to my suitors? It could cause talk, you know."

Bean Plant said, "All right, all right! What *is* the matter with you anyhow?"

Lily sobbed. Then Lily whispered the sorrow of her heart. "I think," she said, "that the sun is dying."

"The *sun!*" cried the sisters together. "Lily, you dream up the strangest things!"

"The sun does its duty," said Bean Plant.

"The sun shines on beauty," said Marigold.

"What makes you think it would die?" they demanded.

"He told me so," said Lily.

"The sun doesn't talk!" shrieked the sisters.

"Maybe not, and maybe so," said Lily. "But he is weaker today than yesterday and lower in the sky than a week ago and he doesn't last as long from the east to the west, and this is how he said, 'I'm dying, Lily, dying!'" Poor Lily could barely say the words, and she bowed her head and she wept.

The sisters cast uncertain glances to the heavens, and squinted, and measured, and had to agree. Facts were facts, after all: the sun was in decline.

"Well," said the sisters, "So what? So what if the old bald-head wears out? We'll do right well without him."

"But," said Lily, "I love him. He watches me. Oh, Bean Plant, how could I live without him?"

"Lily, don't be a nincompoop!" said Bean Plant. "The sun is not a somebody, and that's that. Now, you'll excuse me; I've work to do."

And work she did.

Bean Plant began to preserve her abundance. She dried it and packaged it, wrapped it in tough skins of tan and yellow as long as witch's fingers and hung it on branches above the ground, and these were her pods. "Because," she said, "I don't need the sun after all. I've got my wit and my work and my health. All on my own I am a very important person. It's neither here nor there to me, if the sun should go away." Busy Bean Plant! She stored her goods in bigger barns and waited and wished that her sister wouldn't cry.

Marigold, on the other hand, did nothing.

She checked her brilliant golden blossoms. She looked behind her on the ground and perceived a shadow there and said, "I made that." She took note of the posture of the grass, all brown and all bowed down—to her, as it seemed to her—and she said, "I did that." She touched her cheek and found it warm. And upon all the evidence she concluded that she did herself shine as brightly as the sun, that she was her own burnished light, "and therefore," she said, "tut-tut to the sun. It's time that I were radiant alone and free from competition. I am a very important person." Beautiful Marigold! She patted her hair and waited for all the wood to acknowledge that she was a knockout indeed, and she wished that her sister wouldn't cry.

It cast a shadow on their repute.

But Lily was helpless to stop her tears. For the sun sighed daily, daily weaker than the day before. And when the sun sagged into bed on a distant horizon, saying, "Good," poor Lily whispered, "Bye." They said "Good-bye" together. Lily knew the truth.

And the deepest truth of all she knew, for the sun was very great, and the sun had told her: all would die in his passing. Not one would be left alive. And as strange as it may sound, Lily accepted her death right readily, even gladly, thinking that then she would not be lonely when he left.

It was a murderer coming, said the sun, as cold a killer as ever roamed the earth, stark terrible in his deeds.

For this reason alone could Lily make herself say "Bye" when the sun had said "Good."

But when she told the sorrowful news to her sisters, they said, "Tittle-tattle, Lily," completely unmoved, because they said, "No one would kill the one who does her duty as well as I," and they said, "No one would dare destroy such beauty," and they said, "We are very important persons after all."

So Bean Plant labored righteously.

And Marigold primped most blithely.

And Lily wept for what was to come; poor Lily wept alone.

———◆·◆———

Once more before he left her, the sun spoke a word to Lily. It was a word of the morning and one that he had been speaking all along, but it had never been so important to Lily as it was now, and she had not heard it so clearly before. Perhaps she had been too young before and innocent; perhaps she had not yet hurt enough to *need* to hear it. Truly, it made her no less sad, for the sun was dying indeed. But it stilled her heart in the middle of sadness, and she ceased her tears and she fell silent. The word was "Again."

But Lily was always different from her sisters, untimely, so they thought, and stupid.

For now that she was quiet, they were shrieking.

The Family Fowl that fed from Bean Plant were thinning drastically. And when she asked them what had become of their relatives, her good friends, they rose on the wind crying, "Murderer! Murderer!" and flew south as swiftly as wings could take them. And when they ceased to come altogether, then poor Bean Plant believed them, and she began to shriek.

The wind that once had dallied with Marigold, dancing round her blossom, now ripped from the north at a terrible speed, frightened by something, snatching the petals from her headdress, stripping her to a most embarrassing bare, careless altogether of his sometime lover. "Look out!" screamed Marigold, trying to catch her colors. "Why don't you stop anymore? Why don't you care to look at me?" "The Murderer," moaned the wind, "so close behind me! Ah, the Murderer!" And when the wind, in his speed, had broken her stem, then poor Marigold believed him, and she began to shriek.

"It's not fair!" shrieked Bean Plant, gone wonderously skinny and shivering. "I've worked all my life, brought bumper crops to everyone, been good, been good, Lord, I've been good! Oh, that should count for something. Not I! I shouldn't have to die!"

"It's okay," said Lily, yearning to comfort her sister.

Poor Bean Plant pleaded, "Then I *won't* have to die?"

"No, you will die," said Lily, "and I am so sad about that—"

And then she wanted to tell her sister what the sun had said, but Bean Plant shrieked, "Then it's *not* okay! It's a *cheat* to someone who's paid her dues—"

But Marigold—with brazen lips—could shriek louder than anyone.

"I don't want to die!" she screamed, as though this made a difference. "Spinster Willows, let them die! Grandma Elms are old and ought to die. But I, I am a knockout! *I don't want to die!*"

"It's okay," said Lily, unhappy for this sister, too.

"Oh, you!" cried Marigold. "What do *you* know?"

"That the sun said 'Again,'" said Lily.

"Your sun is vindictive and jealous!" cried Marigold.

Lily whispered, "He's coming back again—"

But her sisters raised such a loud lamentation that her whisper was lost, and Lily bowed her head, sad, sad, and hating the killer to come, yet very still at the center of her.

And so he came.

The murderer came grey as they said he would—out of the north with terrible robes all around him. And this is how he killed: he killed by kissing.

He kissed Bean Plant in the middle of a shriek and cut it off so that her bones alone stood up above the ground, quivering in death.

Marigold saw and Marigold hid her face in the earth. No matter. He sank into the soil and rose around her roots, froze those, and touched her pretty head, and she was still shrieking "No—" when he silenced her with a kiss. No, nothing stopped him, and nothing protected the living, for he was complete. His name was Winter, dead-white and mighty, hugging the Willows to death, petrifying the waters and rolling the sky in smoke.

Only Lily looked directly at him when he came, hating him, but silently. Only Lily held her peace before he sucked the life from her.

For she had heard the sun to say, "Again."

———————◆———————

Come Easter the following year, there grew a plain, white Lily in the field south of the wood.

For the sun had come and kissed her corpse, and that was how he said, "I love you."

Then the flower had burst a white bonnet.

That was how *she* said, "I love you, too."

The Poet and His Congregation to Christ: Our Beloved, and Our Sweet Communion (John 6:35–59)

Come, touch my lips, my Lord, caress
    With flesh the flesh of me;
One mortal morsel and my "Yes!"
    Shall make me one with thee.
    Come, kiss thee into me.

Suffuse my breathing and my soul
    With sweetness of the wine;
No blood runs hotter nor more whole,
    No scent more sweet, than thine.
    I burn, thy breath in mine.

Then hold me, Christ, a hard embrace,
    The holy arms round me!
Hold, hold me in your body's grace;
    Your Church's unity
    Is my security.

"The Lord be with you." "And with you"—
What salutations here!
But since he melts into us two,
We can, nor do we fear,
Breathe out such spells, my dear.

Oh, all my people, laugh with me!
We have been loved by Christ—
We move, one nuptial company,
His bride by sacrifice,
From here to paradise.
Oh, what a wedding feast will greet
The bride and pride of Christ!

PART TWO

———•———

The Servant of Christ

The Time in the City

THEN JESUS SAID TO THEM, "These are my words which I spoke to you, while I was still with you, that everything written about me in the law of Moses and the prophets and the psalms must be fulfilled." Then he opened their minds to understand the scriptures, and said to them, "Thus it is written, that the Christ should suffer and on the third day rise from the dead and that repentance and forgiveness of sins should be preached in his name to all nations, beginning from Jerusalem. You are witnesses of these things. And behold, I send the promise of my Father upon you; but stay in the city, until you are clothed with power from on high."

Then he led them out as far as Bethany, and lifting up his hands he blessed them. While he blessed them, he parted from them, and was carried up into the heaven. And they returned to Jerusalem with great joy, and were continually in the temple blessing God. (Luke 24:44-53)

To those of you who are graduating,* those responsible for my invitation to speak in this place, thank you. Sincerely. Great gratitude comes of great humility, and I am humbled now—for what could one so close to you have new to say to you? I could wish that I had years on my shoulders, silver in my hair, and wisdom upon my head for an occasion like this. Lacking these, I will give you myself.

---

* These words were first delivered as the commencement address for the graduating class of Christ Seminary-Seminex, St. Louis, 1981.

And I will let the final lines of Luke's Gospel shape my words to you: how the disciples had, before their Lord's ascension, one moment of burning purity; and a gift; and a command.

Pure, for the nonce, was their immediate relationship with Jesus, who stood face-to-face with them one final time. The long struggle of that relationship had come to a sort of climax: hereafter they would not so much witness as *be* witnesses.

Pure, before departure, was the fellowship of those who had learned under the Lord's bright, demanding tutelage. They were yet *they* in the moment; but in the days to come they would scatter as preachers of assorted names, vocations, histories, and deaths.

Pure, too; pure, finally, was the fine conclusion of their education; for now their minds were opened to the Scriptures and to the Christ and to his deeds and to the purpose of their preaching. Exegetes on the edge, they were. Well—it was sort of graduation.

And then—then!—the Lord gave them a gift. Please be careful that you distinguish clearly the gift then given. It was not the power from on high; rather, it was the *promise* of power from on high. The *promise* they might take with them; by the *promise* they might comfort themselves; in the *promise* they might boldly begin to act, because it assured them of the power's coming in its own right time. But they would, nevertheless, go and live and act all with a profound sense of personal weakness, because the promise was not itself the power.

Oh, and the place where they were to go—to stay and to wait in weakness—was also identified by the Lord, for that was his command: in the city. After the fine moment of purity, but before the power yet to come, wait in the city. . . .

My face burned when I was ordained. This is historical truth, no image, no metaphor. My face became bright red and burned.

I suppose the people might have said, "Walt's excited. Look at him blush." It was the end of my two-year education at Redeemer Church in Evansville, under a man named David Wacker. That church had been my school, that man my teacher, and here was the ceremony of endings and beginnings, with music and preaching, lights, flowers, rites, noise, my seat center-front, my self the single excuse for the gathering. "Walt's excited—"

But I knew even then that the excitement of the ceremony was not cause enough for the fire in my face. This was more than mere blush.

Rather, the burning came of this: for once in my long and vigorous struggle with the Lord Jesus Christ, the struggle itself had ceased. For a moment, the relationship had reached a certain purity. At that instant my faith was not being ripped between yes and no, nor my calling ripped between yes and no, as both had been for years. My Lord was Lord and Mine, my calling exquisitely clear—

My faith, you see, was the flame in my face.

And the burning came of this: I sat in the midst of a people with whom I had learned and laughed, talked, failed, and cried; a people against whom I had sinned, from whom had experienced forgiveness, among whom had roared, lived, and loved. And in that instant our fellowship had reached a certain purity, a quiescence of joy. There stood Joselyn Fields—a woman of deep, dark, penetrable skin and flashing white eyes—directing the choir in "Isaiah, Mighty Seer in Days of Old." By her music, her love and her solemnity she touched my lips with hot coals from the altar—

My face burned, you see, with the vital love of the people around me.

And the burning came of this: my education had come to a climax; my knowledge was being validated. My mind had been opened to the Scriptures, and the teacher much responsible was at that moment grinning down upon his charge. To David Wacker, when my vows had been pronounced, to that rangy man at the right of the chancel I walked; and we fell upon each others' shoulders; and we wept; and my face burned.

Three loves brightened my face. The love of my Lord so near. The love of the people so dear. And the love of the knowledge of Christ in words, in Word, and in the holy frame of my teacher.

And still there was more.

Somehow I received that facial heat as a sign from God that he would send his Spirit upon my ministry. This is the truth. I said to myself, "I will remember that my face burned. I'll save this sign." The promise of power from on high. I was content.

But then came Monday, and the ceremony passed; and the music, the moment, the light, and the brightness of my face all faded, resolving themselves into a memory. I began my ministry at little Grace Church, inner city, twenty pews, a tiny study but twice the size of the desk in it, and plaster cracked and dusting that desk.

It was a good thing that I had promised to remember the promise. I was about to need it, because instead of experiencing power, I experienced, more than anything else, The City.

My first sermons seemed to me possessed of a certain nascent power. I preached, I thought, with vigor. And I was particularly gratified to note that Sunday after Sunday bold Joselyn Fields would bow her head behind the organ, nodding, rubbing her chin, meditating. This was a lady of stark determinations, an ebony will, and a forthright honesty. What she did not like, she did not pretend to like. What she liked received her nod and her attention. And if I had captured the organist with my preaching, why, then there was no one I had not captured.

Yet, curiously, she never mentioned my sermons to me when the service was done.

There came the Sunday when I chose to direct my preaching altogether to her. I mean, I looked at her where she nodded behind the organ. I sidled toward her, away from the pulpit. I smiled. I peeped overtop her organ—and behold! The woman was reading music—nodding, meditating, selecting the offertory.

Preachers can feel very lonely for want of an ear.

"Mrs. Fields," I said at the end, "what did you think of the sermon?"

She sized me with a narrow eye and decided to state an opinion. "I know preachers," she said, "who make loud noises to the Lord. Please do the same. I can't hear you."

I was in The City.

Grace was an all-Black congregation, except for me. During that first summer of my ministry racial tensions ran high in Evansville, and higher, until riots broke out around the church. I suffered anguish at the news because I lived, then, at some distance, but my own people were caught in the turmoil, cordoned behind police barricades. Worse, I wavered at what to do; they hadn't taught us Riot in the Seminary. Finally, I clapped my collar to my throat—some sort of a badge, at any rate—and prepared to drive to the thick of the threat, to be Pastor in the crisis or else lose my rights of pastoring altogether.

But the telephone rang. It was Joselyn Fields.

She said, "You're not coming, are you?"

I said, "I have to."

She said, "Stay home."

"Why?" I said. My ministry, don't you see? My ministry was at stake.

"You'll get cut," she said.

And I asked, "Why?"

"Man," she said, "because you white," and hung up.

I was in The City.

I was in the common lives of common people: *that* was The City. And I had not yet earned the right to speak an effectual, respected word to the people in their communities, according to their most worldly affairs. That was a higher degree yet to be earned; and it took time.

Neither had I learned the language of The City or its laws, its history, traditions, the triggers of its power, its manner of marketing not only goods, but goodly emotions, ideas, anger, love, complaints, and compliments. That was an education yet to be obtained; and it took time.

But The City was a cold shock for one whose face had burned. For The City reduces the witness. No longer glorying in fine fellowship, the witness is one alone. No longer glorying in knowledge, the witness feels a very stupid sort. In a word, the witness comes up most power-*less*.

How terribly, terribly important, then, that the witness sent into The City remember the promise of the power to come!

———◆———

And now you.

This is a blessed night, a right holy ceremony, your graduation.

Glory is warm in this place. And I don't know; some of your faces are burning. Surely, you are not wrong to smile, or to laugh lightheaded in the occasion, to glow!

Because three loves have come, tonight, to a certain climax and to a moment of unwonted purity.

Your minds have been opened to the Scriptures, to the acts of God in his Christ, to an understanding of the drama of repentance and forgiveness. Your education is at plateau and judged by this very ceremony as Good! Your teachers sit behind me, smiling. The whole process of learning stands still an instant, pure. It is a good thing.

And look at you! You sit center-front among community: classmates among classmates, who have suffered, studied, laughed, talked, and grown together, who have hurt and healed one another; graduates among family and friends, a vast, supporting fellowship of the saints. Pure are all relationships in this peculiar moment. It is, after all, a glory to make a face to burn.

And your faith! After so much rising and falling in the past; after so much struggle with your Christ, denying him and crying after him; after the days when the only thing certain about your calling was that it was uncertain, now comes a moment of sweet truce and unalloyed purity. Jesus sits beside you, and you by him most confident. So lovely is the moment that you want to bark with laughter. Do! It is the right response to glory in this place. And then, remember it.

For these three loves—your education, fellowship and faith—are strings. And God himself doth play upon the strings sweet music. He strums them now, right now, to sing to you a song; and by that song he whispers you a gift. *Not power!* That is not yet the gift. But the promise of power, the promise that power will come in its own right time.

Please, people, remember that it is but the promise of power to come—so that when, by the Lord's direction, you enter The City tomorrow you shall not despair over a creeping sense of powerlessness. Rather, you will say, "This is right. This was to be expected." For the glory of this evening shall tomorrow seem no brighter than a match flame in the common light of day.

But also, please remember that you do *have* the promise, so that you may draw from it both patience and the motivation to do what must be done with your time in The City:

Two assignments by which to earn your higher degrees.

1. Learn The City. Learn the languages of its people, its secular means of communication, the flicker of eyes, the gesture of hands, the postures of contempt, servility, pride, protection, love. Learn The City. Learn the laws that shape it, both hidden in society and open in the books of government. So was Israel shaped at Sinai. Learn The City. Learn its hierarchy, the levels of its power. Learn to read what hurts are real and what their symptoms are. Discover first the human dramas already being enacted in The City before your arrival—for the Holy Spirit is ahead of you, already establishing his work, already directing his purposes. Learning The City, you begin to learn of him.

2. Earn your right to be heard by The City. This is not bequeathed you with your graduation nor even with an ordination. It comes of a very specific labor. It comes when you—to your own

sacrifice—commit your ways to the people of The City; and they shall believe that commitment only over a period of time. Stand with them in the courtroom, if that's where their lives take them; sit with them in hospitals, in jails, in the streets, in their places of business, in their bitter and their brighter moments. It's a hard thing to do, when you feel one and dumb and singularly lacking in the manifestations of faith; but it shall earn you the right to speak when that Spirit gives you the power to speak. It's a hard thing to do; but it is eased and enabled by the promise. You shall have the promise to support you. Remember the promise of power from on high.

For it shall surely happen! By the grace of God, someone's hurt shall find healing in you. And someone's hunger shall, by God's good grace, be satisfied in you. And someone's need shall in you meet solution, all by the grace of God! That moment, that blinding, incandescent, most surprising moment shall be the power come, the Pentecost toward which a long, laborious ministry was tending all along. It shall be. I tell you, it shall be!

———— • ◆ • ————

In the second year of my ministry at Grace, Joselyn Fields fell sick.

In spring they diagnosed a cancer. In summer they discovered that it had metastasized dramatically. By autumn she was dying. She was forty-seven years old.

Spring, summer, and autumn, I visited the woman.

For most of that time I was a fool and right fearful to sit beside her; but I visited the woman.

Well, I didn't know what to say, nor did I understand what I had the *right* to say. I wore out the Psalms; Psalms were safe. I prayed often that the Lord's will be done, scared to tell either him or Joselyn what the Lord's will ought to be, and scared of his will anyway. I bumbled.

One day when she awoke from surgery, I determined to be

cheerful, to enliven her and to avoid the spectre that unsettled me—the death. I chattered. I spoke brightly of the sunlight outside, and vigorously of the tennis I had played that morning, sweetly of the flowers, hopefully of the day when she would sit again at the organ, reading music during my sermon—

But Joselyn rolled a black eye my way. She raised one bony finger to my face. And she said, "Shut up."

God help me!—I learned so slowly. But God in Joselyn taught me with an unutterable patience. I, who had thought to give her the world she did not have, was in fact taking away the only world she *did* have. I had been canceling her serious, noble, faithful, and dignified dance with death.

I shut up. I learned.

I kept visiting her. I earned my citizenship.

And then the autumn whitened into winter; and Joselyn became no more than bones; her rich skin turned ashy; her breath filled the room with a close odor which ever thereafter has meant dying to my nostrils. And the day came when I had nothing, absolutely nothing to say to my Joselyn.

This is as true as the fact that once my face had burned.

I entered her room at noon, saying nothing. I sat beside her through the afternoon, until the sun had slanted into darkness, saying nothing. She lay awake, her eyelids paper-thin and drooping, watchful eyes—we, neither of us, saying anything. The evening took us, and no artificial light went on when the sun went out; but with the evening came the Holy Spirit. For the words I finally said were not my own.

I turned to my Joselyn. I opened my mouth and spoke as a Pastor. I spoke, too, as a human. More than that, I spoke as a man to a woman.

I said, "I love you."

And Joselyn widened her ebony eye. And that lady, she put out her arms. As a parishioner, I suppose; as a woman, to be sure. She hugged me. And I hugged those dying bones.

She whispered, "I love you, too."

And that was all we said. But that, dear people, people, was the power from on high, cloaking both of us in astonished simplicity, even as Jesus had said it would. For in a word that I did not know I knew, a need had found not only its expression, but its solution, too. How dear, finally to hold my Joselyn!

And she died. And I did not grieve.

———◆———

For God's sake, people! When you find yourselves inside The City, know the promise. Remember it. It is true! Not always and always, but in the right moment, in the fullness of its own time, the power shall be given unto you. Let this be peace in your weakness, and purpose in your long routine: it shall be. It shall most surely be, for the mouth of the Lord hath spoken it.

The Making of a Minister

I WISH TO MEMORIALIZE ARTHUR FORTE, dead the third year of my ministry, poor before he died, unkempt, obscene, sardonic, arrogant, old, old, lonely, black, and bitter—but one whose soul has never ceased to teach me. From Arthur, from the things this man demanded of me, and from my restless probing of that experience, I grow. This is absolutely true. My pastoral hands are tenderized. My perceptions into age and pain are daily sharpened. My humility is kept soft, unhardened. And by old, dead Arthur I remember the profounder meaning of my title, minister.

It is certainly time, now, to memorialize teachers, those undegreed, unasked, ungentle, unforgettable.

In memoriam, then: Arthur Forte.

———◆———

Arthur lived in a shotgun house, so-called because it was three rooms in a dead straight line, built narrowly on half a city lot.

More properly, Arthur lived in the front room of his house. Or rather, to speak the cold, disturbing truth, Arthur lived in a rotting stuffed chair in that room, from which he seldom stirred the last year of his life.

Nor, during that year, did anyone mourn his absence from church and worship. I think most folks were grateful that he had turned reclusive, for the man had a walk and a manner like the toad, a high-backed slouch and a burping contempt for fellow parishioners. Arthur's mind, though mostly uneducated, was excellent. He had written poetry in his day, both serious and sly, but now he used words to shiv Christians in their pews. Neither time nor circumstance protected the people, but their dress and their holiness caught on the hooks of his observations, and pain could spread across their countenance even in the middle of an Easter melody, while Arthur sat lumpish beside them, triumphant.

No: none felt moved to visit the man when he became housebound.

Except me.

I was the pastor, so sweetly young and dutiful. It was my job. And Arthur phoned to remind me of my job.

But to visit Arthur was grimly sacrificial.

After several months of chair-sitting, both Arthur and his room were filthy. I do not exaggerate: roaches flowed from my step like puddles stomped in; they dropped casually from the walls. I stood very still. The TV flickered constantly. There were newspapers strewn all over the floor. There lay a damp film on every solid object in the room, from which arose a close, moldy odor, as though it were alive and sweating. But the dampness was a blessing, because Arthur smoked.

He had a bottom lip like a shelf. Upon that shelf he placed lit cigarettes, and then he did not remove them again until they had burned quite down, at which moment he blew them toward the television set. Burning, they hit the newspapers on the floor. But it is impossible to ignite a fine, moist mildew. Blessedly, they went out.

Then the old man would sharpen the sacrifice of my visit. Motioning toward a foul and oily sofa, winking as though he knew what mortal damage such a compost could do to my linens and my dignity, he said in hostly tones: "Have a seat, why don't you, Reverend?"

From the beginning, I did not like to visit Arthur Forte.

Nor did he make my job (my ministry! you cry. My service!

My discipleship! No—just my job) any easier. He did not wish a quick psalm, a professional prayer, devotions. Rather, he wanted acutely to dispute a young clergyman's faith. Seventy years a church-goer, the old man narrowed his eye at me and debated the goodness of God. With incontrovertible proofs, he delivered shattering damnations of hospitals (at which he had worked) and doctors (whom he had closely observed): "Twenty dollars a strolling visit when they come to a patient's room," he said. "For what? Two min-utes' time, is what, and no particular news to the patient. A squeeze, a punch, a scribble on their charts, and they leave that sucker feeling low and worthless." *Wuhthless,* he said, hollowing the word at the cen-ter. "God-in-a-smock had listened to their heart, then didn't even tell them what he heard. Ho, ho!" said Arthur, "I'll never go to a hospital. That cock-a-roach is more truthful of what he's about. Ho, ho! I'll never lie in a hospital bed, ho, ho!" And then, somehow, the failure of doctors he wove into his intense argument against the goodness of the Deity, and he slammed me with facts, and I was a fumbling, lubberly sort to be defending the Almighty—

When I left him, I was empty in my soul and close to tears, and testy, my own faith seeming most stale, flat, unprofitable at the moment. I didn't like to visit Arthur.

———◆———

Then came the days of his incontinence, both physical and reli-gious.

The man was, by late summer, failing. He did not remove himself from the chair to let me in (I entered an unlocked door), nor even to pass urine (which entered a chair impossibly seamy). The August heat was unbearable and dangerous to one in his con-dition; therefore, I argued that Arthur go to the hospital despite his criticisms of the place.

But he had a better idea, ho, ho! He took off all his clothes.

Naked, Arthur greeted me. Naked, finally, the old man asked my prayers and the devout performance of private worship—and we prayed. Naked, too, he demanded Communion. Oh, these were not the conditions I had imagined. It is an embarrassing thing, to put bread into the mouth of a naked man: "My body, my blood," and Arthur's belly and his groin—he'd raised the level of my sacrifice to anguish. I was mortified.

And still he was not finished.

For in those latter days, the naked Arthur Forte asked me, his pastor, to come forward and put his slippers on, his undershorts, and his pants. And I did. His feet had begun to swell, so it caused him (and me!) terrible pain in those personal moments when I took his hard heel in my hands and worked a splitbacked slipper round it. He groaned out loud when he stood to take the clothing one leg at a time. And he leaned on me, and I put my arm around his naked back and I drew the pants up his naked leg and I groaned and deep, deep in my soul I groaned. We hurt, he and I. But his was the sacrifice beyond my telling it. In those moments I came to know a certain wordless affection for Arthur Forte.

(Now read me your words, "ministry," and "service," and "discipleship," for *then* I began to understand them: *then*, at the touching of Arthur's feet, when that and nothing else was all that Arthur yearned for, one human being to touch him, physically to touch his old flesh, and not to judge. Holy Communion: in the most dramatic terms available, the old man had said, "Love me.")

———◆———

When I came to him in the last week of August, I found Arthur prone on the floor. He'd fallen from his chair during the night, but his legs were too swollen and his arms too weak for climbing in again.

I said, "This is it, Arthur. You're going to the hospital."

He was tired. He didn't argue any more. He let me call two other members of the congregation. While they came, I dressed him—and he groaned profoundly. He groaned when we carried him to the car. He groaned even during the transfer from car to wheelchair: Douglas and Clarence and I had brought him to emergency.

But once inside the shining building, his groaning took new meaning.

"I'm thirsty," he said.

"He's thirsty," I said to a nurse. "Would you get him a drink of water?"

"No," she said.

"What?"

"No," she said. "He can ingest nothing until his doctor is contacted."

"But, water—?"

"Nothing."

"Would you contact his doctor, then?"

"That will be done by the unit nurse when he's in a room."

Arthur, slumped in his chair and hurting, said, "I'm thirsty."

I said, "Well, then, can I wheel him to his room?"

"I'm sorry, no," she said.

"Please," I said. "I'm his pastor. I'll take responsibility for him."

"In this place he is our responsibility, not yours," she said. "Be patient. An aide will get him up in good time."

O Arthur, forgive me not getting you water at home. Forgive us the "good time," twenty minutes waiting without a drink. Forgive us our rules, our rules, our irresponsibility!

Even in his room they took the time to wash him, to take away the stink, before they brought him water.

"Please—call his doctor," I pleaded.

"We're about to change shifts," they said. "The next nurse will call his doctor, sir. All in good time."

So: Arthur, whose smell had triggered much discussion in the halls, finally did not stink. But Arthur still was thirsty. He said two things before I left.

He mumbled, "Bloody, but unbowed."

Poetry!

"Good, Arthur!" I praised him with all my might. Even a malicious wit was better than lethargy. Perhaps I could get him to shiv a nurse or two.

But he turned an eye toward me, gazing on this fool for the first time since we entered the hospital. "Bloody," he said, "and bowed."

He slept an hour. I sat at bedside, my face in my hands.

Then, suddenly, he started awake and stared about himself. "Where am I? Where am I?" he called.

"In the hospital," I answered.

And he groaned horribly, "*Why* am I?"

In all my ministry, I have wept uncontrollably for the death of only one parishioner.

The hospital knew no relative for Arthur Forte. Therefore, at eleven o'clock that same Saturday night, they telephoned me. Then I laid the receiver aside, and I cried as though it were my father dead. My father. Indeed, it was my father. Anger, failure, the want of a simple glass of water: I sat in the kitchen and cried.

———◆———

But that failure has since nurtured a certain calm success.

I do not suppose that Arthur consciously gave me the last year of his life, nor that he chose to teach me. Yet, by his mere being; by forcing me to *take* that life, real, unsweetened, barenaked, hurting, and critical; by demanding that I serve him altogether unrewarded; by wringing from me first mere gestures of loving and then the love itself—but a sacrificial love, a Christ-like love, being love for one so indisputably unlovable—he did prepare me for my ministry.

My tears were my diploma, his death my benediction, and failure my ordination. For the Lord did not say, "Blessed are you if you know" or "teach" or "preach these things." He said, rather, "Blessed are you if you *do* these things."

When, on the night in which he was betrayed, Jesus had washed the disciples' feet, he sat and said, "If I then, your Lord and Teacher, have washed your feet, you also ought to wash one anothers' feet. For I have given you an example, that you also should do as I have done to you. Truly, truly, I say to you, a servant is not greater than his master; nor is he who is sent greater than he who sent him. If you know these things," said Jesus, "blessed are you if you do them."

Again and again the Lord expanded on this theme: "Drink to the stinking is drink to Me!" One might have learned by reading it. . . .

But it is a theme made real in experience alone, by doing it.

And the first flush of that experience is, generally, a sense of failure; for this sort of ministry severely diminishes the minister, makes him insignificant, makes him the merest *servant,* the least in the transaction. To feel so small is to feel somehow failing, weak, unable.

But there, right there, begins true servanthood: the disciple who has, despite himself, denied himself.

And then, for perhaps the first time, one is loving not out of his own bowels, merit, ability, superiority, but out of Christ: for he has discovered himself to be nothing and Christ everything.

In the terrible, terrible *doing* of ministry is the minister born. And, curiously, the best teachers of that nascent minister are sometimes the neediest people, foul to touch, unwuhthy, ungiving, unlovely, yet haughty in demanding—and then miraculously receiving—love. These poor, forever with us, *are* our riches.

Arthur, my father, my father! So seeming empty your death, it was not empty at all. There is no monument above your pauper's grave—but here: it is here in me and in my ministry. However could I make little of this godly wonder, that I love you?

Preaching

IT IS NOT INSIGNIFICANT THAT my first apprehension of the love of God was granted in an experience with my father. Nor is it generally uncommon that God is apprehended in experience. Nor, in fact, can the divine and human meeting happen any other way. God is not a God of the pulpit, though the pulpit proclaim him. He is a God in and of the histories of humankind.

What *is* significant is that I should have to say so.

We, the professional faithful, the preachers so earnest for our responsibilities, have measured the arena of God's activity by our own; and the people, glad to be led in definitions, have allowed us to noose the mighty God and to remand him to a tiny space. To a tiny space, a discrete time, and a handful of particular, prescribed exercises. Because *we* meet the people formally from the chancel and the pulpit, there it is that God most evidently meets the people. Because we must necessarily schedule our time, sometimes serving, sometimes not, it is assumed that God operates also on some sort of schedule. Because we make much of pious or liturgical procedure, implying some form, good form, some formula, some proper votive attitude as needful for the manifestation of God, so the people assume that there are rules and requirements governing God's good will and his appearing, and that certain people possess the rights of propitiation, while others do not—but that God is circumscribed by them nonetheless. Moreover, because our own most usual apprehension of the Deity is by a noetic labor—studying, reading, analyzing, classifying, theologizing, propounding and providing *doctrine,* teachings—because our preaching is largely teaching, explaining and instructing, so the people may assume that God is a matter of the mind (or the heart, in more emotional deliveries), but not of the whole human in all its parts. We say, of a text, "This is what it means." And we imply that God comes present in the understanding of meanings, *even though these meanings be pointing to events!* Our manner communicates more than the matter we would deliver, because it is subliminal and qualifies every word we say.

Despite what we may think, and despite the freedoms we experience in so many areas of our culture, we remain, where religion is concerned, a people of the priest. By those singled out for the office we meet and perceive our God: the meeting is a conscious desire; the perception is an unconscious shaping; the consequence, except the priest be careful, is the contraction of God and then God's abstraction from the whole of life.

Contraction has through the ages been an effect of the priesthood, and often a desired effect. The first three strictures mentioned above—to place, time, and the special rites of propitiation—have always bound God to temples, festivals, and ceremony. Evil priests found power in controlling the All-Powerful. And frightened people were happier not bumping into an arbitrary God unawares. But even when fraud and fear were *not* the motives, people believed that the Limitless had found limits and *therefore* was approachable. The priesthood was an order within greater society: God was less than the whole; he was contracted.

Abstraction, on the other hand—an effect of the fourth stricture mentioned above—the removing of God from experiential life and permitting him truly to dwell in the analysis alone, is a present-day problem. To be sure, the Greeks of the fifth century B.C.—those who poo-pooed the historical value of their myths, re-interpreting them and worshiping the wisdom that triumphed over story—had mentalized their gods as well; but these were a clear minority and the rest of the culture continued to offer sacrifice. Today the trouble's more pervasive for two reasons: first, we are less honest than they. We pretend God's presence in the whole of our lives, and we believe the pretence, though in fact we honor understanding. Second, our priests themselves participate in the problem. Because they are also preachers; because so many of us consider preaching to be their most significant function; preaching seems to us the clearest access to the divine. Therefore, the shape of preaching most shapes our God. And what is the shape of so much preaching today? Why, it is the shape of the classroom: teaching. And teaching is always (in our consideration) one step removed from experience and from the "real." It is an activity of the mind. It prepares for what will be; or it interprets what has been; it is separated from both. The God who is met in doctrines, who is apprehended in the catechesis, who is true so long as our statements *about* him are truly stated, who is communicated in propositions, premise-premise-conclusion, who leaps not from the streets, nor even from scriptural texts, but from the *interpretation* of the scriptural texts—that God is an abstract, has been abstracted from the rest of the Christian's experience.

O Priests, by the will of the people!

O Preachers, by the patterns of this age!

O Teachers, by thine own choosing—you have severely belittled the Deity! Though your intent was kind and holy, your manner was mousy. Though you brought extraordinary intelligence, a fine education, and assiduous study to your office, you reduced that office to intelligence, its training and its application alone, and this you made the temple of the Lord.

But the province of God is all creation, all space and time, all things and all events, all the actions of humankind, and all the whole human himself!

Nor does he watch these things and care about them only; he acts within them! He uses them as instruments, the experience of the people. He participates most fleshily. No abstraction, he! He is *not* only transcendent; but by his own will and power he cracks into our histories and there he works his works.

Or what does the psalmist mean when he sings, "He utters his voice, the earth melts"? Or Amos: "The Lord roars from Zion, and utters his voice from Jerusalem; the pastures of the shepherds mourn, and the top of Carmel withers"? That the word of God is more than mere instruction: it has manifest power before the eyes of the people and hard against their hearts. It created. It continues to shape creation in a most palpable way.

Or what does the psalmist mean when he sings, "When thou hidest thy face, they are dismayed; when thou takest away their breath, they die and return to dust. When thou sendest forth thy Spirit, they are created; and thou renewest the face of the ground"? Or John the Divine: "And I heard every creature in heaven and on earth and under the earth and in the sea, and all therein, saying, 'To him who sits upon the throne and to the Lamb be blessing and honor and glory and might for ever and ever!'"? It means that both the rule and the necessity of God are presently over and through *every living thing,* visible things, classifiable things, analyzable things—but it is not in the analysis of these things that his power works; rather, in the things themselves.

Or what does Jeremiah mean when he calls the pagan Nebuchadnezzar "the servant" of the Lord? Or what does Isaiah mean when he claims the pagan Cyrus to be anointed of God? They take for granted that the finger of God is in the affairs of *all* humankind, that it requires not somebody's faith to be touched by God, but God's will, God's choosing alone. God chooses *both* to be manifest in human history *and* to direct that history as well, for discipline and for mercy.

Or what, for heaven's sake, is the incarnation, if it doesn't announce God's personal immersion in the events—the bloody events, the insignificant and humbly common events, the physical and social and painful and peaceful and daily and epochal events of the lives of the people? In their experience! And isn't the coming of the Holy Spirit the setting free of that immersion, so that it be not restricted to any sole place, time, or people, but breathes through *all* experience and temples in *every* faithful breast?

Of course. Of course. It is not hard to argue the immanence of God. Why, it is one of our doctrines.

One of our doctrines. There's the sticking point. So long as it remains a doctrine alone, a truth to be taught, immanence itself continues an abstraction—and is not immanent. God abides not only in the church, but in the books in the church, and in the minds that explain the books, and in the intellect.

What then, Priests? Preachers, what shall we do that the people's perception of God not be so much less than God himself?

Make something more of our preaching. Allow the preaching itself a human—and then a divine—*wholeness:* that the whole of the preacher be presently active in proclamation, the whole of the hearer invited to attend, and God will be seen as God of the Whole.

Or, to rush the point: tell stories.

The preacher is not a mouth alone, self-effacing that God alone show through. (When that is the case, then God is a mouth alone, and that is *all* of him that shall show through.) The preacher in all of his parts is the proclaimer of God: his wonder, his humor, his faith, his body, the tone of his voice as well as its words, his *experience!* The entire drama of his own relationship with God, both in sinful enmity and in holy forgiveness! Her husband, if she be a woman, is part of that proclamation, and her children. His parents, his wife, the leaks in his roof, his surgery, his pains and his pleasures, his troubles and their resolutions. Three times in Acts the story of Paul's conversion appears, twice in his own mouth. It comes again in Galatians. His aggrieved experience threads the letters to the Corinthians: the message of Christ is proclaimed not only by Paul's intellect or teachings, but by his very being and in wholeness! He may be embarrassed by boastfulness; but he does it anyway, and so God is seen in lashes, in prison, on a ship, in dreams—everywhere immanent.

I tell you of Arthur Forte, and behold! God's in the squalor; God's in a hospital; and by a naked, obstreperous man, God is shaping me like a clay pot. I tell you of Joselyn Fields, and God explodes in the common language between a man and a woman. I tell you of the day my Matthew forgave me, and Jesus Christ walks through the doors of one man's study, to ease his burning guilt in the cool blood of the cross. Doctrine may judge the rightness of my perceptions; doctrine may name the details of the event and caption them like pictures: "sin," "repentance," "forgiveness," "justification." But I stand before you in flesh and blood; I risk the disclosure of myself and my experience; I present you with the very stuff itself of the events that have shaped this person before you, and so reveal the Shaper shaping. By these stories I am sinfully, gracefully *whole,* and whole may be the drama of God in me. (I do no more than St. Augustine, then, do I?) Like Cyrus to the Jews, Arthur Forte is anointed of God to set me free. Like Isaiah of the Scriptures, I *say* so: and God appears immanent in human events. I am more than a preacher. I am myself the preaching. For God chooses to touch me whole, not only in my mind.

Oh, no! There is no pride in such personal revelation—not unless it is sinfully conceived. For the complete drama of God begins with my rebellion and ends with his forgiveness. Remember St. Paul's repeated story? How could either Paul or I find personal glory in what amounts to confession—confession of sin, confession of faith?

Tell stories, ye preachers of God. Humble yourselves to make of yourselves a parable.

Because when you do that, you invite, as well, the wholeness of the hearers. Then not only their analytic minds, but their laughter shall be in the pew; and by laughter, their lungs and their consternation; their bodies, their sympathy, their emotions, their distress, their inadequacy, their male- and femaleness, their parenthood—their experience! You will be inviting them as *people* (not only as students) into a relationship with you. For if once they laugh, or cry, or remember their own past week, or nod—just nod—then they are using more than their minds, seeking more than understanding. To you, who offered your Self, they are returning their Selves. A teacher calls to students, and intellect to intellects. But a whole person calls to people, and to answer is to allow wholeness, too, in that relationship. There's the word: such preaching encourages human *relationship,* and so, love.

And then—if it is in such a relationship that God takes up his dwelling, he dwells in the wholeness of the people's histories. His temple is their experience. They shall know him immanent, indeed. Nothing is not the stuff of a story. All of the senses participate. Then the pulpit is only a place to stand, and the whole world is seen in a word, and the Word in the world.

———•◆•———

I told stories in university classes—
　　—and football scholarships cared to hear what I had to say.

———•◆•———

I told stories to my children—
　　—together we named their bogeymen, their wordless terrors, and we were allied against them, since my children listened while I spoke, and so they were not alone; and they dealt in imagination with the hazards of their imagination—it is where they live and solve problems; and they laughed; and the story *became* the power! And the story became the vehicle not just of an affectionate love, but of a medicinal, transfiguring love. And my children triumphed.

———•◆•———

I told the story called "Lily" to my congregation—
　　—Mary Ellen Phillips, who heard it then, told it to her niece

in Nevada, who suffers from muscular dystrophy, and the niece chuckled to hear it. But when that niece's friend died in a cruel accident—a boy sixteen, as she was, with whom she was in love— none could comfort her, not her parents, not her pastor, none. But Mary Ellen went into the bedroom where the child was crying, and prayed God for words to say, but had none. But then her niece said, "Tell me 'Lily'—"

———◆◆———

If the story of Jesus Christ took place among the people, then the preaching of Jesus Christ must also find place among the people; and since story involves the people whole—enticing personal commitment by the desire to hear the ending—it is story that can plant it there. It is not doctrines that comfort us in crisis. Nor are crises like examinations in school, attention to one isolated problem divorced from reality. It is Jesus himself who comes to comfort us, and crises are the dramas that swallow us down whole, as the fish did Jonah. The stories *of* experience (themselves becoming experiences for the hearers) prepare the people to see God approach them *through* experience.

"I don't want the doctrine of resurrection. I don't even want the promise of resurrection. Please: I want the *calmness* of resurrection. Tell me 'Lily.'" Or one might say, she wanted the kiss of resurrection, which was, just then, the kiss of Jesus, the hand of him who bestrode two worlds at once, the one in which she had to dwell, and the one that had taken her friend. "Remind me: Tell me 'Lily.'"

———◆◆———

What were the Saints' Tales in medieval tradition but a high and finely popular form of preaching? And story.

And what were the stained glass windows, and the stations of the cross, and the biblical paintings (all in the dress and the landscape and the face of the times *in which they were crafted*) but visible forms of preaching, and the translation of the Christ into their own experiences? And story.

And the finest Black preaching of this century and the previous three does precisely the same thing—tells the stories of Christ in black-face, and of Israel according to Black experience. Or else, volte-face, it tells the story of its own people, and behold! Jesus walks in. No mystery to that: Jesus *is* the mystery.

Martin Luther King, Jr., begins his proclamation "I Have a Dream" by referring to a small experience he had with a small girl; just as St. Peter begins his sermon to Cornelius with reference to the experience he's just had among Gentiles; just as Jesus seats little children on his lap or remembers a traveler from Jerusalem to Jericho—

Out of experience rises the Word in order to lodge in experience once again. And story is experience communicated. Story is Word and experience abiding each within the other.

———◆———

If Jesus began a sermon by saying, "There was a man who had two sons"—

—O Priests! Why mayn't we do the same?

Now, this is the truth: I first knew the love of my God in the love of my father.

I used to get dreadful cases of poison ivy. Angry red dots spread my limbs, erupting in bunches like mountain ranges. On my face the pustules ran an amber fluid that scabbed in amber crust. And it went into my hair, my nostrils, the backs of my hands, and so forth. Fierce cases and most debilitating itches. I was miserable.

I was also convinced that scratching the stuff spread it; so I schooled myself in stillness. Awake I could hold a position before the TV set for hours at a time. Sleeping, however, I lost control and would wake both scratching and on fire. So I conceived a plan. I had my brother tie my hands behind my back before I went to bed—with ropes, belts, the bathrobe cord, tape, anything. But nothing worked. I was Houdini in my sleep, slipping the most intricate knots of my brother and scratching hell out of my flesh, I, my own assassin!

So, my mother conceived a plan. She'd heard somewhere that Fels Naptha soap was a warrior against the itch. She had *not* heard that laundry soap is supposed to rinse the skin of ivy oils within an hour of touching it; rather, she considered it a lotion. Therefore, my mother, who didn't do things by halves, worked wonderful lather of Fels Naptha and applied it to every mass of rash on my body, and so it dried, and so it caked, and so her son was mummified. It's hard to sweat under a cast of Fels Naptha. Worse, the stuff was stiff against my skin, so every move I made irritated a thousand dots, which all set up a jubilation of itching and drove me to a pitiful distraction.

More than ever, I schooled myself in stillness. I lay on my bed all the day long and thought that this was the way I would end my life.

On a particular afternoon, when I'd brought my flesh to quietness, was lying perfectly still abed, my father came into the room and sat beside me to talk with me—matters of the world, and so forth, before the dinner I would not share with the family, and so forth.

It was a nice talk. He is a kind man. I didn't move or look at him. But I could hear his voice.

Now, there are certain places on a boy's body that, try as he might, he can't keep still. On that place on my body, there was, at that time, one poison ivy dot. And that bodily part began to move. So that single poison ivy dot began to itch.

This was more than I could take. In a moment, all the plans of the world and all the remedies failed. Life was very bleak. Without turning my head, without so much as a sob or a moan, I began to cry. The tears trailed down my temple and pooled in my ear. I thought that I would die soon.

But then I heard a strangled sound to my left.

It was my father. He'd risen to his feet. His hands were up and empty. His face was so full of anguish, seeing my tears, that my own heart went out to the man. He turned, turned fully round in the bedroom, seeming so helpless; and then he bolted for the door, crying "Calamine lotion!"—hit the wood and left.

Calamine lotion. I was experienced in the ways of poison ivy. I knew that calamine lotion was utterly useless even if it could get to the rash; but *my* rash was covered by a rind of Fels Naptha soap. No good. No good.

Nevertheless, when my father appeared again with a giant bottle of the stuff; when my father knelt down beside the bed, uncovered me, and began so gently with his own hand to rub it on; when my father's eyes damped with the tears of suffering, so that I saw with wonder that my pain had actually become *his own pain* and that it was *our* pain that had sent him rocketing to the drug store; when I saw and felt that miracle, a second miracle took place: the ivy did not itch.

Calamine lotion did not do this thing!

My father's love did this thing—and I knew it! Oh, my heart ached to have such a father, who could enter into me and hurt so much that he took my hurt away.

I was a special child that day, abed and still and watchful. For this was the love of God, incarnate in a man with a receding hairline and a patch of whisker on his chin and a smell I shall never forget.

Whom was I naked before? Whose hand made miracles against my skin? God. God's.

It was here I first began to discover the mercy of God and such magnificent preachments as "Vicarious Suffering." And it was here I learned that love was no word, but an event, a sacrifice.

But as yet I knew none of the phrases, nor the *theou logoi*.
Simply, I had experienced the power of God.

———◆———

I tell you the story, dear brothers and sisters, to say—
—tell stories. It is the fullness of witness.

A Christmas Pastorale

CHILD, YOUR MOUTH IS TURNED DOWN. There are weights at the corners of your lips. And something's squeezed your forehead together; your brow is plowed as deep as the soil, and the winter has frozen it so.

What are these weights? What makes you frown?

Ah, look at you. Your shoulders sag, and hands droop, and knees are bent. Deep sighs, I hear them. Deep sighs blow from the basement of your soul—

Come. Sit. Talk to me.

And, lo: you talk. You shock yourself with talk. You roar.

I think you did not know how visible was your sorrow nor how great the pressure within you, so my sympathy ambushed you; my eyes dropped your defenses. And since my eyes do not look away, grief rushes out of you—words, words, memories, accusations, reasons for your desolation, reasons by the score whirl like blackbirds in the room, making you dizzy with their number: you did not know you had such reason to be sad. You did not know you were so full of complaint. In spite of yourself, you cry. You roar on account of your tears, angered by them as well as by a God-damnable world—until the tears choke you and you jam your face into toilet paper, because I had no Kleenex, and now you don't wish to show your face again—

And I listen.

What I do, I make you a cup of coffee, very slowly, clacking the spoon on crockery to let you know that I am busy *not* staring at you. You need the time and a hollow space in which to meet yourself. This cup of coffee is my gift to your dignity. Here. Sugar? No? Then, here.

You take the cup and do not drink. You press it against your cheek—for the warmth, perhaps: it is a bitter winter. Your elbows on your knees, gazing at the floor, you begin once again to talk—humiliated, I think, for having lost control. I notice that you make whole sentences, now, attempting some popular psychoanalysis for yourself. I do not smile at you. You are no psychologist, so your explanations ring cheap and partly pompous; but the effort is earnest and touching: you are struggling to prove self-mastery after all. I do not smile.

I listen.

My Lord, how carefully I listen, for when will I get this chance again? I don't know. In a thousand ways I signal listening: I nod. I purse my lips. I say, "Oh." I squint recognition of a trenchant point. I cover my mouth, pull at my chin, lean forward, watch closely the dark, flitting center of your eye, which steals glances at me—

I listen. And I hear, finally, that all of your sorrows are one sorrow only.

Oh, it is a terrible sorrow, to be sure, and fierce and able to hurt you horribly. But it is only one. You have divided the one into many, because it shows itself in a thousand forms, all of them hiding their source. And you have accepted the *many* as your problems because you do not want to acknowledge that single source. And why? Because the source is in you. No, the source *is* you. And that would be a hell of an admission. With all my heart I understand that: we would rather suffer a hundred troubles caused by other people than admit one for which we alone must bear responsibility. That would be suicidal, wouldn't it? Then nothing whatever of worth remains. But the suicide, don't you see, occurred at the beginning of sorrow, not at the end of it—

And I love you, child. I love you.

———— • ◆ • ————

Therefore, when you have finally fallen silent and are liking the silence I lend you, when you sip once or twice my cardboard coffee and sigh and wonder whether the pastor minds cigarette smoke, then I take a breath fearfully and I begin to speak.

Fearfully: because I do not take your side against dogs and the bulls of Bashan. In fact, I'll seem somewhat to set my eyes against *you*. Fearfully: because I am going to tell you the truth that you've been so diligent to hide. It's a surgery. But now—right now while the thing is warm between us, and all the evidence is on the floor—you are vulnerable to the truth. Right now, before you lid your eyes against the cigarette smoke and forget that you cried and dress yourself in hard habit again; right now the pain might trigger change instead of anger. And when will I get this chance again?

I draw my breath and say, "Oh, why did you ask the Lord to leave your life?"

You shoot me a glance, as though I'd changed the subject a little too violently; but I haven't. Your nostril flares, as though you sniff a dangerous tack; there you are right.

"Don't you understand?" I ask. I am whispering. "When you sent Lord Jesus away, you sent your strength as well." You lower your eyes to my chin. I've said the name twice, now. Had you hoped I was a pastor above pastoring? Real people?

I speak very low and very fast: "When you dismissed the Christ, you denied the Cause for Joy. Therefore, you lost the cause for honest smiling (though the smile still clutched your face awhile, so you didn't connect his leaving with your losing it). That's where your shoulder's droop comes from, old friend, and the weights at your lips and in the heart of you. Friend of mine— why did you choose to become your own law, your own Lord, Master of your own existence? You are no good at it. Look at you.

Look how you have failed. If the pitch goes bad, don't blame the bleachers. Blame the—"

"Pitcher!" Your word: snapped to show I'm not ahead of you. But the second cigarette's too quick upon the first. Your soul is squirming. I suspect that you are seeking reasons to dislike me, to judge me, or, at least, to scorn me. You could devalue my words that way. Or else you are pitying my poor preacherly ignorance, my unworldly idealism, making me too inexperienced to know the truth.

But I love you, child, and I persist.

"Not me," I say, "but the Lord. It is the Lord himself who is unsettling you right now. Not me, though you can't look me in the eye. Not me, who seems to be betraying our years of friendship by God-talk. It is the Lord you wish to avoid. Perhaps you're scared of his return? You think he'll come to judge you? No, it's worse than that: you think that you will die at his coming, see all the furniture of your life destroyed, the delicate balance against the void. Well, in this last," I whisper, leaning forward, "you are right. Masters die at the Master's coming—"

Now you are absolutely silent. Your gaze has jelled, like cataracts; and though you look toward me, it's nothing of me that you focus on. You are making no commitments, not with your eyes, not even the least of commitments, which is that you might be listening. Commitments, I think, terrify you. They wear black hoods and hide their faces and could, in the end, behead you.

Oh, I want to cry for you—so tough, you! You swagger like the children mimicking their elders; but *you* are the elder, mimicking children! You, your only, foremost enemy. You, you, for *your* sake, won't you look at me?

This is the hardest time for me. I truly do not know whether I am winning the moment or losing it. Your face shows nothing: no sorrow anymore, for that was vulnerability (dear to me, to you so dangerous), no hope, nor joy, nor pain, nor friendship. Nothing.

I want to cry for both of us. Because I love you—

Therefore, in a voice as clean as its message, laundered of my feelings, I persist. (Lord, let my words be like the snow to him!)

"For God's sake, do not be afraid," I say. "His coming is going to lay you waste, yes. But it will not hurt you in the way you think. He'll come into you the same as first he came into the world: Christmas, old friend! A baby conceived and growing. That's how he enters you.

"Hush, hush, hear me," I say, but I do not touch your knee. You've made it a block of wood. Are you cursing yourself for confiding in me? "It begins in delight," I say, "as when a man and a woman make love together, only, it is God and the people to-gether—"

You mutter, "Penetration," and I laugh out loud. That you talked at all is something. And I'll take your word as a joke. You can't demean my metaphor, because that's precisely what it is—

"Penetration! Right. And you, old friend, are the woman who can do nothing but cease to deny it. You drop your arms, two weapons once against the Love, both muscle and bone. All un-protected you lie before the mighty God, helpless under the Holy One. Penetration: I like that. And then the life introduced by this sweet joining is small and hidden in the depths of your being. But it is there, there, independent, powerful, alive inside of you, and growing.

"And then your mind will sometimes go inward to the baby's turning. 'Ah,' you will sigh at odd moments, grabbing your heart, 'something kicked.' You'll close your eyes to comprehend the miracle: God in you. And the world that watches you will wonder at your silent wondering. They'll say, 'What's come over you?'

"See? This is the first stage of his coming into you again. Christmas.

"But then the parturition, the birth, old friend. Not forever can the Christ stay hidden inside of you, but he will be born into your open life—with labor and pain on your part, to be sure; but with the shock of joy as well: He is! He lives! This is what he looks like, whom I have loved silently, who was in me, but who was ever before me.

"He will live visibly in your deeds and in your doings. Baby pieties will receive from you a trembling attention, a worried, yearning watchfulness. Your language will change. The people will look at you and see a new thing and demand its name, and you will say, 'Jesus,' and they will go away wondering still; but you will smile as any mother would.

"This is the second stage of his advent here: Christmas.

"Finally, he will grow as children grow. He will mature until he is revealed as stronger, broader than you and wiser. Then, old friend, the pain is past, when him you *thought* the infant stands before you as the Lord, and you admit *yourself* the infant once again. Then the pain is past, when you confess how asinine you were to master your own life with such another Master by. Then it is he who lifts your hands and strengthens your weak knees and straightens out your walking, who smoothes your brow and gives you life again and raises up your slack lips to a smile. If first you died in his conception. If you surrendered to the dreadful penetration—"

I am leaning forward. I do not want to stop talking, because, when will I get this chance again? But the words are gone out of my mouth, now, and next I'll repeat myself, but my heart is hammering the repetition already: did I say it right? I'm a little breathless. For two minutes together I struggle to control that, then notice that the intensity of my stare embarrasses you.

That's wrong. I shouldn't embarrass you.

Like a lover compromised, I drop my eyes. I put my hand on my mouth. The snow is stroking the windows. Your cigarette has made a two-inch ash that droops like an eyebrow. It's dead against the filter; the filter's between your fingers. It's quiet here. There's an empty sanctuary outside my door. *Shoosh* says the snow. And you are saying nothing.

It's up to me to set you free, one way or the other, *one way or the other*. That is to say, I have to signify when our conversation's done. You won't. You wait. You've chosen only to endure.

Dear God! What have I done to you?

I whisper, "*Christmas*, child."

And that is all.

You rise immediately. "Merry Christmas to you, too, Pastor," you say, and "Where do I put the cup?" It's full of coffee. You thank me. You are very much collected, now, and no one would know the rip in your soul that I knew one hour ago. Did I get through before the stitch? You are blank. I can't read past the blankness: snow in a frozen field. You shake my hand, and then you leave me, and I hold your cup.

Ah, I pray as you go. With all my heart I pray that you are *not* giving me a fine show of independence, that you have *not* chosen to "deal with my problems alone," the master of your soul and well shed of the wimp, religion. Earnestly I pray that you are going out to meet your Christmas, that acute conception, that laborious birth, life—

But I don't know, after all. I can't tell. All I've got right now are your boot tracks in city snow, and even those are filling. I have to wait long, long, to see the evidence of Christmas in your face. But I will wait. I will wait. Child, I will wait a lifetime. Because I love you.

A Minister for the Nations

I SAW ZEPHANIAH KOMETA FOR the first time in the lobby of a Seattle motel, where I'd been waiting for the car that would take both of us up to a mountain retreat. We were scheduled to lecture. We might have been equals, except for our races and his great-hearted humility.

Zephania (he pronounces it Zeph-AHN-yah) appeared in the door of the tiny lobby, paused smiling, then stepped to the registration desk and spoke. It was curious—it would have been painful, except for that smile—how the clerk reacted to him.

The Reverend Kometa is African, a pastor, a theologian, a citizen of Namibia. He is black in every respect except one: his skin is white. He was born an albino. So his kinky hair is straw-yellow, and his eyes are hurt by sunlight, and his flesh shows the scars of sun-sensitivity. He stands tall and angular. He keeps his head bowed to the ground. Gently does the man smile; gently does he move; and gentle is the timbre of his voice. His accent is soft and African, requiring of his American listener a particular attention for understanding him.

Zephaniah Kometa asked the clerk for a newspaper, smiling, casting his half-blinded face down to the counter.

The clerk raised her own eyes and uttered the first half of the word "What." The clerk said, "Wha—" saw Zephaniah's face, snapped her mouth shut, and began rapidly to blink her eyelids.

Zephaniah repeated his request more clearly, nodding in order to send it to this woman with gentle nudgings.

The clerk popped her mouth open and began to giggle.

She broke sight from the man before her. "I," she said. She frowned at her fingernails. "I, hee-hee, hee-hee."

"Nyews-pepah," Rev. Kometa said.

The clerk peered anxiously about the little lobby, seeking help. And there was I. Her face suffused friendship and familiarity, and in a whisper shouted: "What did he say? What's he trying to say?"

But I had never met the man before.

The African reached, touched the back of her hand, and pointed to the magazine rack: the newspapers.

His touched snapped her still. His gesture triggered understanding. In a sudden haste to grab the paper, she swept her pen and registration papers to the floor. He bent to help her. He served her.

And I wondered who the man might be, so restrained, refined, patient, dignified, and kind.

And, at first glance, so odd: a black man white; a white man black.

The clerk—relieved when our car arrived—never would know. But I had a week with this remarkable minister. I came to know.

———— • ————

Presently Dr. Zephaniah Kometa teaches at a seminary in Namibia. In those days he was the pastor of a parish under South African rule, if indirectly. In those days South Africa's rule was hard, by apartheid distinguishing fiercely among Blacks and Mixed and Whites. Both the pastor and his people knew oppression in their flesh. They suffered arbitrary "detainments," imprisonments without formal charges; suffered impoverished opportunities and circumstances; suffered the severe restrictions of their freedoms, their travels; suffered the fears and the hatreds of a ruling white minority. They had few rights that they could count on, plan upon, build a future and hope and identities upon.

Rev. Kometa himself, as a leader, lived daily, consciously, with the knowledge that he could be murdered. He is younger than I am. In those days he was younger than I was—and I was forty-one.

After the lecturing, after chats at mealtimes and pipes in the evenings—in the night before we would descend the mountains together and part and return to our separate ministries—I sought him out. The wonderment that had begun for me in the lobby of a Seattle motel had in six days only grown deeper. I knew what he was about to do. But I didn't know quite why. I wanted to know his motives, and something of his heart.

Therefore, I met him late in the evening, in the dark that made similar colors of us both. We sat outside on a high porch, he in a chair, I on a step. And the great starry sky was the ceiling above us.

———◆———

"Zephaniah," I said.

"Walter," he responded. *Well-tah.*

It was, I thought, not unlike the conversations of the Old Testament which begin "Samuel," and continue, "Here am I."

I said, "You're going back, of course. It goes without saying, doesn't it?"

"Going . . . back?"

"Yes. I mean to Namibia."

Zephaniah's eyes are wide open at night. If he ducks his head then, it is out of habit, not for any need of protection.

"Namibia," he said, looking directly at me; then he tossed his head up and laughed. "Well-tah," he said, "what would my wife say if I did not?"

I, of course, was thinking of the circumstances into which he would return, and I spoke the next words almost as if they were a confession: "You are," I said, "a brave man. A courageous man."

His laughter turned into a hoot. As if I'd told a right fine joke.

I cleared my throat.

Zephaniah bent and touched my shoulder.

"Oh, no," he said. "Oh, no, there is no great courage in me, Well-tah, I assure you. Listen: where we live, our houses are not so tightly closed as yours. Animals come creeping in at night, sometime for the warm, sometime for the crumbs. But if it is for the warm, then I hear them, you see. I hear them rustling under our bed. And *then*, Well-tah. . . ."

The African paused, shuddering with laughter, patting my shoulder in clear indication that I was not the cause of it.

"And *then* I pretend with all my might to be asleep. Oh, yes, so deeeeeeply asleep. For you know, Well-tah, that soon my wife will wake up. And she will hear the slippery creature under our bed. And she will say, 'Zephaniah! Zephaniah, get up and kill that thing!' But me, oh, I am sleeping, sleeping, and can no one wake *me* up—because I am scared to death of little creatures at night. Nooo. No, my wife would have a big argument with you, Well-tah, about this assessment of her husband: courageous."

"Then, Zephaniah," I asked of his laughter, I think, and of the pure melody of his humor, "then do you go home with some fear? Or with none?"

He sat back in his chair, a presence above me.

"Fear," he said soberly. "I go to my home and my congregation always alert with fear, which is a good and necessary fear. But it is a much more dreary fear I carry within me quietly."

I commented on fear then, since I felt it likewise in my own inner-city ministry. But I drew comparisons and simply could not find words for the oppressions that caused his. My life was not in danger.

"But you go home," I said, as if no conversation had passed since my first comment and this.

Zephaniah suddenly raised his right hand high above the both of us, blotting out a thousand stars.

"For my friends," he said.

I was quiet. It was not unreasonable for me at that moment to envision the members of his congregation, his colleagues, his relatives, the "friends" for whom he put himself in harm's way, being a leader—and my sense of friendship was enriched thereby.

But I was wrong.

"My friends," said Zephaniah Kometa, "are in desperate need, are in the soul's need, and perhaps none but we, black and Christian, can save them."

"Your friends, Zephaniah," I said.

"Yes?"

"Your friends are . . . white?"

"Yes. Of course. White."

"They . . . your . . . I'm sorry, but do you mean that these friends are your *oppressors?*"

"Who are themselves far more oppressed than I. Far more imprisoned and miserable."

Rev. Kometa spoke these brief declarative truths without drama. They were the facts of his existence. His ministry. And mine.

"Well-tah, they may be the ones who oppressed me and my people. But they are visible, you know. It is the invisible that oppresses them. It is sin. And who shall set them free from sin?"

"Zephaniah, can you tell me truly that you don't hate those that hurt you? Truly? You are scared of them, but you don't hate them?"

At that question—that appeal, really—my friend slipped from his chair on the porch and took a seat beside me on the step. He bowed his head, and now it was the cloud of his hair that caught starlight and the stars themselves in fiber like a crown.

"You see," he said, "they are not the enemy. They are threatened and wounded and killed by the enemy of everyone. This enemy is killing their souls. He can only take my body, not my soul, not my life. So they are under the worst oppression. I do not hate them. I pity them."

"Then who is the enemy?" I asked. Yes, I knew the answer to my own question; but I had never before met the minister who could utter the answer with the whole of his being, his body and his choices and his actions and his will and his faith—not just with his mouth alone.

"Who?" I asked.

"Evil," he answered. And he gave evil a name, for it had in Africa a personal presence, a power, and a violent purpose: "The enemy is the Devil."

———◆———

In Africa. In America. Wherever souls might be divided between life and death, evil is not people! Evil is not our first and final kin, the grand scattering of the children of Adam and Eve. Our deepest enemy never was, nor ever will be, those who kill the body, but after that have no more that they can do. "But I will warn you whom to fear," said Jesus to those he called *friends*: "Fear him who, after he has killed, has power to cast into hell. Yes, I tell you, fear him!"

The servant of God, therefore, is sent by God to serve whom?

Joseph served those that had sold him into slavery.

Jonah (in spite of himself, my colleague-ministers!) served the city of the "enemies" of his people, Nineveh of Assyria. In the name of God, he served those who would murder Israel; and by God his ministry was successful, for these people repented that they might be saved.

Hosea served her who had left his marriage bed to share her prostitute's bed with many instead of one.

Jeremiah served those who scorned him, despised him, imprisoned him in a muddy cistern.

The servant of God is sent, therefore, to serve whom?

Jesus Christ ministered unto all people.

In Jesus there is no division of the peoples. For didn't he supercede enmities by urging his disciples, salt and light, to replace the old command, "You shall love your neighbor and hate your enemy," with his new command: "But I say to you, Love your enemies and pray for those who persecute you, so that you may be children of your Father who is in heaven."

And though the Christ of God approached his most horrible act of ministry with fear, praying the Father to remove the cup from him, he nonetheless finished the act and saved the people.

For the enemy is the Devil, the Father of lies, that Evil that would bind the souls of us all and cast them into Hell.

God and the Devil make, between them, a unity of us all! And the true war is cosmic, after all, whether we serve in Africa or America or the city or the ghetto, in wealth or in poverty, in one or the other of the nation-states that have declared (a lesser) war on each other.

In the Reverend Zephaniah Kometa I met a model of the minister who serves the human population *wherever* there are divisions: a minister unto the nations, yes, though his most focused ministry is to the patch surrounding his house. For don't the nations meet there? Right there?

And right here?

———— ◆ ————

And if any should say to me, "But the task is impossible! Enemies will never eat together," I will answer with the story Zephaniah told me, whence his very particular (and most common) method of service.

He said that one day he saw two white children wandering through his neighborhood, obviously hungry and lost and helpless. He did not know how they came to be in a territory altogether black, but he surely recognized their hunger. Spontaneously, he invited them into his house and into his kitchen for food.

Now, Zephaniah's wife was a strong-willed woman who harbored in her bosom a fiery anger against white people. She had many proofs of why the blacks *should* be angry. She was also the only cook in the Kometa household.

When her husband entered the kitchen with the two little white children, she was facing away from them, busy with a soup.

He said to her, "You must give these two small people something to eat."

Still without looking, she said, "Okay. Sit down, all of you," and she ladled soup into two bowls, and then three, and then (Zephaniah was glad to note, for it meant that she, too, would sit with them) four. Except for her anger, she was a woman of kindness.

When she turned holding two bowls, she saw that the children were white.

Zephaniah told me that he ducked but kept watching her face.

"Oh, Well-tah, it was *then* I felt fear, fear in the gravest category."

The woman's face snapped shut like an iron pot. With shaking motions she set the bowls down, one before Zephaniah, one before an empty chair, none before the children. She turned back to the soup and paused a while. Then (Zephaniah said it was for no other reason than civility) she took another bowl and turned and placed it at the chin of one white child, turned again and again did the same for the other.

She did not sit.

But already the children were spooning the soup into their mouths, fearlessly, sloppily. They were so hungry that they took no notice of the drama occurring about their heads. They wanted only to eat. They made much noise, slurping, breathing, sucking.

And as the children ate—by the very act of their eating, the simple human need being satisfied—Mrs. Kometa was softened. She could not watch these hungry children, whom she herself was feeding, and remain angry. The hunger made them citizens of her own country, for its name *was* Hunger, and she had lived there a very long time. Moreover, it was her hand and her soup that now was nourishing them, which made them, too, the children of her own motherhood.

Before they were done, Zephaniah saw his wife touch the corners of her eyes with her sleeve.

This is why the African theologian would stoop in the lobby of a Seattle motel to serve a baffled, belittling clerk.

"When someone serves some other one out of kindness alone," he said, "the first one cannot hate the second one for long. When a woman feeds the children of her enemy, she discovers in her heart that they are of her flesh too. She discovers that she has shared motherhood all her life long with the mothers of these children. And then how can one find the fires for hating still?"

Servants of the Cross

FINALLY, I AM CONVINCED THAT we are not called upon to succeed at anything in this ministry. We are called upon to love.

Which is to say, we are called upon to fail—both vigorously and joyfully.

———◆———

For the sake of ten righteous people, God does not destroy the world. These are the Lamed Vavnik. They live scattered, in any nation under heaven, are members of any class, of any profession which may be imagined; and they are invisible to the world. Lo, not even they know the significance of their lives. Such ignorance *is* their righteousness. They merely live, so they suppose, as other people live. But Heaven knows the difference.

And this is the mercy of God: that when one of the Lamed Vavnik dies, God raises up another.

I heard this from my friend. He said it was an old Hasidic legend.

I believe it.

PART THREE

The Body of Christ

Rachel

"I'M JUS' LOOKIN' for my grandbabies. And maybe you seen my grandbabies?"

The old woman's voice whines in my mind at odd times, grieving me, urging me, who can do nothing, to do some little thing after all. Oh, the humble supplications are the most horrible, since they enlist the conscience, and it is the conscience that echoes forever until I bend and put it to rest. "Woman! What, what between me and thee?" Conscience. Common humanity. The heart's language commonly spoken, and you speak it, and I understand it, though I do not always choose to understand, but we are members of the same Body, various extremities, and I am commanded to understand—

Woman, hush!

I will do something.

I will name you Rachel; and I will magnify your cry by writing it; and with it I will fill the ears of the people.

———◆———

At eleven o'clock on a Tuesday night I left and locked my office, then stepped into dark night and a thin drizzle. Oily concrete in the close and cratered city. When I slid into my truck, both my hair and my feet were damped—and my spirit. I sat utterly still awhile, tired.

It is not unusual, at the end of the day, quietly to wish for endings absolute and to nurse the dream.

But then I heard what sounded like a wailing outside the rain's whisper: "Hoo-ooo. Hoo-ooo."

Cat's call?

No, it was a high, broken, desolate voice, as though someone cried "Please, please" without words. Two simple notes, high and low, one simple song. But I saw no one, and I would have thought it the noise of my own weariness, or distant brakes, except that it became insistent, and when I opened the truck door, I heard it the louder: "Hoo-ooo! Hoo-ooo!"

It came from the alley that dead-ends at Gum Street. Louder, and yet infinitely patient.

"Hoo-ooo!"

Then a bent figure emerged from the alley, stood at the mouth of it, and the wailing turned to words: "They ain't bad boys. It ain't that they is bad, oh, no," she said. "I'm jus' lookin' for them, you know. But these old eyes is dim, and I cain't seem to see them no ways." She turned aside and raised a hand: "Hoo-ooo!" She turned to the other side, like the poor picture of an orator: "Hoo-ooo!"

Talking, she was. But there was no one, absolutely no one, near the woman, neither companions to hear her talk, nor grand-babies to come at her call. She was alone.

I stepped from the truck, winking against the mist.

Street-light glinted on her face, gnarled, wrinkled, deep-dark and harder than black walnut. She wore a man's vest and a man's shoes. Her eyes jerked left and right, so intent on the search that she didn't see me. She was a tiny bit of woman.

"It ain't no time," she said full reasonably, "it ain't no place for them to be about. And it's a dirty, weathery night. Hoo-ooo! Hoo-ooo!"

Who was she speaking to? God? The eyeless night? But her purpose was so inarguably right that I couldn't leave her now; and it was clear that love and yearning together had driven her into the rain.

I coughed.

"Hey, Mon!" She saw me. "I'm jus' lookin' for my grandbabies."

She came immediately and clutched my arm in a bird's claw,
her head at my chest. I smelled her tight, neat hair. Raindrops
hung from earlobes pierced and ripped a long time ago. She was
not ashamed to look me in the eye. "And maybe you seen my
grandbabies?"

"No, I don't think so," I said, though I wished with all my
heart that I had. I thought of brown infants potching in puddles.
"How old are they?"

"Oh, they be strapping big boys," she nodded, holding my
eye. "Each of him could give a head to you, Mon." I'm six one. So
they were big, these boys. They didn't need me.

My wish to assist her melted in the chilly drizzle.

But the lady was earnest. Her fingers had sunk between muscle and arm-bone. "How long," I asked, "have they been missing?"

"You gonna look?" she demanded, bright old eyes drilling mine.
She reached her other hand to my cheek.

"Well," I said lamely—she was buying me by touching my
cheek—"yes—"

"Ooo, God bless you, child!" she said. "They been gone two
lonely years, now, and I'm thinkin' they hurt, Mon, and I'm feared
they be troubled. Oh, Mon, you help me to find them!"

Two years! I spluttered in the manner of educated people
whose education is meaningless before the bare, forked animal.

"Mon?" She drew down my face so that I had to look at her.
"Yes, ma'am?"

"It's a promise? You use the powers Jesus given you? You be
helpin' me to find them?"

She had no teeth. Gums black and a darting red tongue and
lines at her eyes that enfolded the soul.

I said, "Okay."

Immediately she released me, forgot me standing there, and limped down Gum to Governor, a tiny and tinier bit of woman: "Hoo-ooo! Hoo-ooo!"

———— • ◆ • ————

Mad, I thought driving home and dripping in the cab of my truck. Ho, ho, crazy lady! Midnight's citizen!

And despite my vow I tried to forget her desperate, patient, weary search for grandbabies.

But I can't, you see, forget it. Like spasms of conscience her voice keeps recurring inside of me. Certain sights, certain sounds trigger the cry, and I groan to remember her face, black walnut shell. Neither rain nor the late, exhausting nights do this to me, though one would think so by association. Rather, it's a moral memory.

Listen, and I'll tell you when I hear the pleading song, "Hoo-ooo."

When I see young strapping men slouch into Bayard Park beside my house—

They carry beer cans low at their sides, and bottles in packages. They drink, they laugh unmindful of anyone else, they gaze with vacant eyes to the void-blue skies, they leave a most unsocial mess behind. And compulsively I wonder with the crazy lady's sweet irrationality: Are these her grandbabies? These, the handsome, strong, and lost? Do they know what they have done to her? Can't they hear the old woman's call, "Hoo-ooo?"

So much for intellect and my education. The woman's infected me with madness.

Or, when I smell the strapping young men in front of my house—

Smell, because their car windows are open, and the acrid smoke of marijuana cannot be disguised. "Hoo-ooo!" And they gather in front of Doc's Liquor Store, those who could give a head to me, those beloved of an old and searching woman. And they park at

the Eastland Mall; and they ride wild on the North Side, the East
and West sides in loud careless cars; and they live in a thousand
homes throughout the city, great weights upon an already crippled system, strapping youths who have chosen to live according
to their own desires alone, full of their own boredom, forgetful.

"Is that old lady your grandma?" I want to say. "Don't you
know that every private choice that you make for yourself is not
private at all, but hurts her? Don't you know that she still is looking, a singular figure in the night, still is looking for you? There
are no private choices. There is no such thing as 'your own thing'!
All selfish action damages those in love with you!"

No. The lady is not mad. She simply has a love that will not
quit against reality—and that only looks like madness. She is
Rachel.

"A voice was heard in Ramah, lamentation and bitter weeping. Rachel weeping for her children, and she would not be com-
forted, because they were not."

Oh, go home again, you strapping, slouching youth, so full of
promise, so full of yourselves! Bow down before mad, merciful
Rachel. Ask her forgiveness. Then give her love for love.

Clara Schreiber

I.

I RECEIVED BY MAIL A formal invitation, a careful calligraphy written on pasteboard and signed with a flourish: "Walter Wangerin the Third," it said, "be pleased to lunch with me in my home, sir." A date and a time were attached, and the whole was signed, "Clara Schreiber."

Sir? To whom was I anything *like* a "Sir"?

I knew the woman, of course. She attended the church where I functioned as an assistant to the pastor. She was old, and older than I knew—a woman of dignities toiling up the aisle toward the chancel on the arm of her daughter, which woman herself was more than sixty years old. At her left hand, then, her daughter Ruth; with her right hand, however, Clara Schreiber leaned on the walking stick she alone controlled; and motion caused her joints to tremble; and a vagrant air caused her white hairs to wave, so silken were they; and I, sitting in the chancel mere minutes before the worship service began, I could see the front of the woman, poor eyes peering through corrective lenses as heavy as lake ice. When she sat, when we sang, she would fix her vision upon some mote in the middle distance between herself and the cross behind me, and she would sing and she would pray and she would confess with the rest of the congregation all from memory.

These are the things I knew about Clara Schreiber, all of it gathered from the public encounter.

What I didn't know was why she would invite me—or why she would make such a to-do about it. If she wanted my ministering, a phone call would have done as well. But she had requested nothing at all of me during the whole year I had been serving Redeemer. I was young. I had not yet finished my seminary training. In fact, my service at Redeemer was fulfilling the internship year required for my graduation—after which I would be ordained. Not me: it was Pastor David Wacker who ministered to Mrs. Schreiber.

Me? I was responsible for education in the church, for the youth, for a host of lesser duties, necessities in a large congregation but mostly invisible. By day I did my job with competence. By night I gave myself backaches, hunching over an old upright Underwood typewriter and writing stories and rewriting stories. . . . This for me was a compulsion. Forces deep within me drove me to write, to improve my writing—"forces," you see, which, since I could not control them, caused me to feel secretive and ashamed.

Once, several years earlier, I'd sent my parents what I considered to be the manifesto of my future and my purpose: *I have decided,* I (a graduate student in English) divulged with some fear and trembling. *I want to be a writer.*

My mother was the one who responded. *Good, Wally!* she wrote. *Write greeting cards. There's money in greeting cards.*

It was the formality of Mrs. Clara Schreiber's pasteboard invitation that confused me—and that assured my obedience—for it implied some honor, some value in the young intern which he himself could neither discover or believe in.

———•◆•———

I was surprised by the house. Perhaps the invitation had put me in mind of something stately and Victorian. Instead, the Schreibers lived in a small bungalow, green shutters framing the two windows, one to the right and one to the left of the front door.

Ruth met me, smiling, took my "wraps," and led me back from the tiny front room through a hall into the kitchen.

Ruth was afflicted with a muscular malady. She walked with stiff concentration and slight noises in her throat. She carried my jacket in the crook of one arm and with the other gestured to her mother, Clara Schreiber, crouching on the far side of a little table. "Vicar Wangerin has come to see you, mother," she said, and I saw the older woman's head snap in my direction. It was unnerving. Ruth withdrew with the jacket, while her mother pierced me! The blind old woman under silken filaments, weightless waves of white hair, pierced me with an ancient, milky eye.

I sat.

She never took her eye from me.

Even sitting, she leaned right-handedly on her cane. She crouched, exactly as she did walking, and I realized that age had broken her upper spine like a reed, that the woman crouched perpetually, of necessity.

"I am so pleased," she said, "that you agreed to visit me in my home. Are you comfortable, Walter? Are you content, sir, in every particular?"

Sir: spoken as well as written.

I said I was content, though her blindness made me feel as if our conversation passed through a glass of mystery and that she, after all, set the terms of it.

Mrs. Schreiber said, "You have met Ruth?"

"I—" I began.

But Ruth herself startled me, having returned without my knowing. Standing at the stove she said, "Yes, mother. We have met."

"Then these are my introductions," Mrs. Schrieber said. It felt as if we were ambassadors gathered at some high summit together. "First, Ruth. She is my amanuensis."

I had never in all my studies met that word before: *amanuensis.*

"She sees and reads for me. She is my hands to write my words on paper. Second, Walter Wangerin, Junior. You, sir, are an author."

Wait! What had she said? Shivers shot up my back. She said that I was an *author*. I did not, nor had I ever, felt worthy of such a title. But how did she even know?. . .

Mrs. Schreiber didn't even pause.

"You, sir, are an author," she said. "And as for the third member of our small communion here, I will introduce myself in a moment. Please, let's eat."

We ate. Rather, I ate. Ruth served. Blind Clara watched. It was a full German meal at noonday. But how could I, under her bluish eye, say no to second helpings of mashed potatoes?

With dessert, Clara Schreiber spoke again.

"I have invited you here for three particular reasons." Her bird-claw-like fingers clutched the knob of her cane. "One," she said, "I am renewing old acquaintances. I knew your grandfather, sir, and I loved him much. In the 1920s Reverend Walter Wangerin was the pastor of the same church where my husband was principal of the parochial school. Lombard, Illinois. Your father was but a boy. You see, sir?" She produced a wintry smile. "I stride across the years to greet you from your generous and gentle grandfather. He and my husband respected one another. They labored well together. If you are half the first Walter Wangerin, you'll be twice the measure of most."

When people spoke well of my grandfather, I was always inclined to sink to my knees and pray profound thanksgivings unto God for such an ancestry. But that feeling was immediately superceded by the stunned rush of joy which Mrs. Schreiber's next revelation caused in me.

"My second reason," she said, "consists of my own introduction. As I have published a small volume of my own, I am an author like you. I wish you to know this regarding me. It is good for those of a common interest to recognize one another."

An author! Oh, this took my breath away. I knew no authors in those days. Authors dwelt in my hungry Olympus, reverenced but out of reach. Yet here! Why had no one told me this marvelous thing about Clara Schreiber.

"You—" I whispered.

"Patience," she interrupted my admiration, "for my third reason demands that we be realistic—and requires of you, sir, level-headed thinking."

She paused. It was only then I realized that the trembling of her joints had been increasing. Her cane twitched for the bending of her elbow.

"Walter," she said softly, "I offer myself to you as a mentor. If you wish it, if you will accept it, I would walk with you a while. But please," she held up a cautionary hand to my grinning enthusiasm. "Please, take time to decide. An elder author can perhaps inure a younger to difficulties before they arise."

Did she truly mean *inure?* To prepare me to meet things undesirable? It's like inoculate. What possible wrong could come of publishing a book?

Clara Schreiber suddenly leaned forward, piercing me to the seat of my trepidations with her gaze and her next comment:

"But do accept, Walter, for you should never, never be forced to dance in the dark. No one should. No, not ever."

And so our first meeting came to an end, and I was dismissed, my latter mood somewhat more subdued than my other moods had been: so premonitory her yearnings that none should "dance in the dark." I had no idea what she meant.

She gave me two books upon my departure. Neither was hers. One was, rather, a biography of Mozart, and the other of Chopin.

And of course I accepted her proposal. That which ratified my secret life?—which brought legitimacy to my private compulsions?—how could I *not* graduate to this next level in my education?

But, as much as I admired the woman, I confess I did not

accept the proposal with the veneration it deserved. It was only as the weeks went on and we worked more closely together that she began to disclose herself to me. I learned her story piece-meal, and only then realized how extraordinary was my good fortune. What Mrs. Schreiber (the "Writer," as the German name implied) knew of writing, I quickly came to equal. But what the woman knew of charity and sanctity and sheer endurance, I shall never equal. Great Church, we ought to canonize such women for their outrageously loving spirits, for their suffering, and for this: that they could translate pain not into vengeance, but into blessing.

I give you my Matron Saint, whose mentoring was my epiphany.

2.

Even from her childhood Clara Schreiber was compelled to write. This was no choice. It was what she was. And while she was young, in the last decade of the 19th century, people generally tolerated her curious hobby. They could, you know, tolerate the fancies in a child that adulthood and marriage would finally shake from her. She would soon be schooled in the more proper duties of a woman. She would conform to the role society prescribed for her.

And Clara was no fool. She knew precisely what these expectations were. But neither (she reasoned) did she have to cease doing what still could be done in secret—so long as her church, her community, and her family were kept content by her happy accomplishment of every other duty. Therefore, even after marrying Teacher Schreiber, Clara continued to write. But no one read what she was writing.

She raised her children. She protected her husband's reputation and her own. And she did dearly respect my grandfather's person and his ministry. Her daughter Ruth went to school with my father Walter. And all was well. There were no scandals.

Clara wrote when the children were sleeping. When they grew old enough to attend parochial school, she wrote in the afternoons while she had the house to herself. She wrote in perfect solitude, however deeply the writing longs a reader.

For these were the presumptions on that society: that writing was fine for students and essays and sermons and postcards; but *creative* writing, so-called, was a frivolity. And for women—conscientious women, Christian and Lutheran women, pious women—creative writing was considered vainglorious, a vanity to be censured, a self-centered dereliction in wives and mothers, a sin or else the sign of that womanish malady: hysteria.

This is not to overstate the case. For though the church could be as civil as a Sunday suit, it knew exactly what pieties were required of its people, and in a thousand ways how to shame the impious.

But Clara Schreiber wrote, and that's a boldness of spirit I can scarcely comprehend. She wrote. She must have been like Spanish Moss, surviving on air. She survived, though her identity was buried inside of her. She wrote; and what's more, she began helplessly, devoutly to write a book.

This is what the old woman told me about her younger self: that in the autumn of a particular year, after having spent much time in her own researches, she began with deliberation to write an actual volume.

In the mornings she finished the housework. All the chores that were hers to do she cleared from her lists and from her conscience. In the afternoons, then, she sat at the dining room table and produced—page after page in a flourished longhand script—a biography of Katherine Luther. The wife of a Lutheran school teacher was honoring the wife of the fifteenth-century reformer. She described this work to me by the image of fire. "Some coals," she said, "I kept bright in my soul for Kitty and the book. Although the greater fire burned in the furnace of our house, a part of me was always dwelt in the closet of my work."

By the following spring, Clara finished.

She had been storing the written pages in the box that had brought them blank. Now, she told me, she sat at the dining room table sealing that box and (she giggled over the memory) wrapping the box with a delicate blue ribbon. She packaged the whole and sent it off to one of the few publishers she knew, Muhlenberg Press in Philadelphia, Pennsylvania.

And then she waited.

Quietly she passed the summer, hearing nothing, saying nothing—but she could not douse the coals.

Then came September. And then October. And then the letter.

The thin envelope arrived from Muhlenberg Press late one afternoon, too late for a woman to sit and read it because her children were already halfway home.

Clara could have plucked her anxiety and her excitement like the strings of a violin, astonishing her household by a Godawful noise. She didn't, of course. She waiting the evening out, and the night. In the morning she made a point of cleaning the kitchen. And only when she was done with that did she sit down at the dining room table for this: to read the letter.

She slit the envelope. A single folded sheet was inside. This she withdrew, spread open before her, and read.

Mrs. Clara Seuel Schreiber, the publisher had written her. *It is a fine manuscript. We will be pleased to publish it.*

"Walter!" Clara Schreiber said to me, "I wanted to cry tears, just as though they had written, *No.* I wanted with all my heart to rise up laughing.

"Oh, Walter, I folded the letter with two folds again, and I slid it back into its envelope, and I touched the envelope with the tips of my fingers, and I thought I would pray a thanksgiving, but I could not! I could not! Instead, I stood up. And I pressed my hands hard on the top of my head to keep it from exploding. And then I started to turn around. Round and round I twirled, faster and faster, until my skirts ballooned and my arms were high in the air, and I was dancing! I was dancing! Oh, Walter, my hair flew backward and I cried for joy to God in heaven—and I danced that day as I had never danced in my life before!"

Suddenly Clara paused in her glad recitation of this joy, and she was old again in front of me, trembling upon her walking stick and blinking rapidly.

Softly, she said, "But before I allowed such dancing to overtake me, Walter, I went to the dining room drapes, and I pulled them closed so that no one would witness my joy. No, no one should witness such vanity."

In consequence, Clara Schreiber, author, splendor, God's bright eye—she danced. . . .

"I danced," she told me. "But I danced in the dark."

3.

"I offer myself to you as a mentor," Mrs. Schreiber said.

And I accepted her offer. And I thought it was in the craft that she would mentor me. But in was in the spirit, after all. In the Holy Spirit. And in the deepest sense and practice of the Gospel.

For the woman had every right to judge the church for its sins against her: the unconscious sins, the sins of the character of the times and of the people being its worst sins, since there is neither recourse nor repentance then. None dare blame this woman if she had fed her survival with a strengthening anger, or else preserved her soul by a contemptuous separation. In my generation I have witnessed such actions as the genuine liberation of women from these nearly killing oppressions. For them salvation was surely in Christ and through Christ in God, but not in the visible church.

But Clara Schreiber handled the sins against her differently. She was never descended into ignorance. Blind, she never blinded herself to the truth of her situation. And what she did, she did by *choosing* it, not by fear or forcing or capitulation.

In the last chapter of Genesis, just after their father has died, the brothers of Joseph are filled with fear that he will deal with them the same as they dealt with him years earlier, binding him and selling him out of the family into the hands of slave-drivers. Joseph has become powerful, second only to the Pharaoh in Egypt. The brothers fall down before him, begging forgiveness.

Joseph says, "Fear not, for am I in the place of God? As for you, you meant evil against me; but God meant it for good, to bring it about that many people should be kept alive."

Let me be clear: God did not cause the sin that severed Joseph from his family. Neither is God responsible for the oppressions that society and the visible church have imposed upon women such as Clara Schreiber. Nevertheless, it is through the actions of these persons, a Joseph and a Clara, that God comes most truly present to people like me, for in them the sin stops cold and mercy goes forth like warm coals instead! And this is an act of pure grace, since it is not required of Joseph or Clara Schreiber—is not required of any whom the church or this society oppresses—to forgive their oppressors! They are under no *obligation* to transfigure sin into mercy; if they were, it would simply be one more oppression upon them, the oppression of a *law* that commands them (forces them, threatens and frightens them) to obey by forgiving.

"So do not fear," Joseph finishes his response to the brothers. "I will provide for you and your little ones."

Which is precisely what Clara did for me! What a holy conundrum! A marvelous contradiction: rather than spend her life in bitterness, she chose to provide me with companionship and with knowledge. She preserved this young and callow writer from the effects of the sin that had buried her; she preserved a mere stripling from the greater blindness of our heritage. Is not this a wonder?—when all the world expected otherwise from her?

Here, then, is the genuine Body of Christ! Here is the Spirit of the resurrected Redeemer active and breathing among us, in this woman, in this saint!

Surely, great church, in the brightness of such saints we can see and confess our sins against women, our demeaning of any who do not fit our easier categories, our dead-weight pressure upon lightsome spirits. Surely, in the sunlight of my Matron's epiphanies we need not darken others hereafter. Surely we will recognize the personhood of each and each, for then and there is the body of Jesus made visible. In God's name, surely!

———•◆•———

And when I was, finally, ordained; and when I was installed as the pastor of little Grace Lutheran Church in the central part of the city; after the blessings had rained down upon my head from fellow clergy, pastors, bishops (in those days mostly male), I looked up and saw, sitting in the back-most pew of this little sanctuary, Clara Schreiber, piercing me still with her milk-blue eye, piercing me as with the point of a spear.

She saw me then too; so I say, laying my hand upon my heart. Nothing in me was hidden before me. In fact, this ordination placed me outside of that church denomination in which I had grown up, the church body in which Redeemer and all its members, including Clara, held membership. I was now in violation of the express demands of the Lutheran Church Missouri Synod. All that is another story for another time, of course—except for the following detail.

After worship, as people filed past me down the steps of the narthex, there, at that crack beginning of my ministry in the city,

Mrs. Clara Schreiber appeared, stopped, turned, took hold of my hand, and held it long in both of hers.

"Walter," she said softly, so softly I almost could not hear her. "Walter, whatever else you leave, you must never, never leave our good and perfect God."

Body of Christ,
You're a Woman

THE PAIN OF CHILDBEARING IS NOT ONE AND ONCE.

It is twofold; and it comes twice; and I am astonished by the love revealed in such a miracle.

Twofold: There are two kinds of suffering that attend the physical bearing of children into this world. The first is that a woman must make space in her body for a baby; and doing that, she sacrifices a host of personal goods: her shape, hormonal equilibrium, energy, her freedom to sleep in any position, beauty (so she sometimes feels) and, with these, her self-esteem.

Did I call such sacrifice a suffering? Well, it is, I suppose. But the wonder is that such suffering also contains the sudden spasms of joy, and that both should come together. The woman who groans is the same who laughs to feel life within her—and I am astonished.

Then, the second suffering of bearing children is the opposite of the first. Having made space for the baby, she must now empty the space. It does not matter how much she has invested in carrying the child. At the end of nine months she's asked to give it up, to separate herself from it, to deliver it whole and squalling into existence. "Go out of me," her muscles say, her womb, her leaning forward, her very self says to the infant: "Go out of me, in order to *be*."

And this is suffering. (The work is so hard.) Yet this also contains the sharp spasm of joy. (Here is life!) And I am astonished that two such things can be together.

———◆———

Twice: Any reasonable person might think that once through this curious drama of love were enough. Once to labor at making room; once to labor at emptying it. But the mother is asked to do it all over again.

For now the child is not in her body, but in her life.

Again, she sacrifices a host of personal goods to give the child the space in which to grow. Her schedule is broken a thousand times by his untimely needs. Her energies are divided. Her sense of accomplishment is shattered every time she does the laundry without gratitude, because it is an endless task endlessly taken for granted. ("Hey, mom! How come my pants aren't ready yet?") Her hair hangs in her face so often that she sees herself unbeautiful; and when she puts it up, she is still not called beautiful; rather, she is called to question: "Why did you do that? Are you going out tonight? Who'll watch over us?" She grows tired. She goes to bed early, and her husband says, "What's the matter? You sick or something? Don't you want to be with me anymore?" And so she makes space for her children. Beauty she sacrifices, and freedom, and with them, self-esteem.

Suffering, did I say? Certainly. Yet at the same time—and this is too high for my understanding—it contains the sudden spasms of joy. She laughs to see her child's emerging life, his walking, his talking, his raking the leaves, his baking cake alone. How is it she can do both?

Then, for the second time, comes the second suffering.

At the child's maturity, she must birth him not out of her body, but out of her house and into the world, an independent being.

It doesn't matter how much she has invested in raising him. By stages, now, she labors to let him go. By degrees she loosens the reins, knowing full well the dangers to which she sends her child, yet fearing the greater danger of clinging to him forever. And now her hurt is the hurt that *he* will encounter on his own. (Will he survive in a careless existence, and thrive?) And beside that, her hurt is loneliness. To *be*, he must be *gone*.

This is childbearing at its most laborious.

On my first day in the first grade, I panicked and cried and raced back to the car where my mother was, ran at top speed before she drove away from me.

"Mama! Take me home!"

I thought she would be so happy to see me and to discover my undiminished need of her presence, her love and her protection. I sat smiling in the front seat and heard the car's ignition even before she turned the key. She never turned the key.

Only now do I understand her own tears as she took my hand and walked me back into the school again.

"Mama, do you hate me?"

"No! No, not at all. I love you—"

What she was saying was, "Go away from me—in order to *be*."

————◆————

So here I am, all done with first grade and writing books like any independent adult, and it is done. My mother sorrowed in the separation; but I am, by miracle, her joy and her accomplishment. Both. It is an astonishing act of love.

They made the Divinity male, and according unto that gender I experienced him. But when they spoke of the creating and the re-creating love of that Deity, their words slipped to the abstract and degenerated into thin, analytic theologizing. *That* love was left to my intellect, but my heart could find no handles for to hold, and my heart hung helpless in a void. I thought of a pot-

ter, and I was a pot. I thought of the dust of the earth, and I was
still a pot. It is hard to imagine life as a pot, impossible to experience it.

On the other hand, they allowed the Church to be the
Holy Mother—and there they struck a chord, and there they
found warm-blooded memory. This story I know very well by
experience—

God mothered me into being in the first place: "This Great
God," sings James Weldon Johnson,

Like a mammy bending over her baby,
Kneeled down in the dust
Toiling over a lump of clay
Till He shaped it in His own image.

The "He . . . in His own image" is a chilly calculation; engi-
neers and sculptors do the same, and the result is steel or stone.
On the other hand, the "Like a mammy bending over her baby"—
that I remember! I have been the object of such love. And the result is blood and bone. At my mother's breast do I discover more
wholly the creating love of God.

And then, within the Church I was protected for growth,
nourished, fed on supernatural food, clothed in a white robe, and,
on my confirmation day, freed to speak my personal faith in God,
in a voice not the Church's but my own. It was *urged* that the voice
be my own! So the Church made space for me. And then the
Church delivered me face-to-face to God. In-and-out of my
mother's house do I discover more wholly that re-creating love
of God.

What other story should I tell to convince the people of the
generative love of God than that which is told by my presence
and my being? For I was born of the womb. And what other story
would strike more nearly the root of their deepest memory than
that which speaks of arms and the babe? They were *all* babes,
once.

Body of Christ—though Christ in the flesh was a man—you, you I remember as a woman, and my mother!

I suppose that it is the Lord's prerogative to make his Body also his own Bride—an androgyny so startling as to be difficult, frightening, and therefore ignored.

The Self to the Self,
and the Fusion

(Strophe)
The trouble with atomic bombs
    Is lethal egocentricity:
When one remarks upon himself
    There goes the near vicinity.

(Antistrophe)
But let me tell you this: my vanity
Build bulwarks all around my sanity.

Killing by the Little Cuts

THIS URINAL CAN'T SWALLOW the cigarette someone flicked in it.

Saddest, wettest, shreddingest cigarette butt I ever hope to see, for the moisture that swells the tobacco's not water alone. And the filter's a sponge. And tendrils of brown bleed across the porcelain.

Sad cigarette, indeed. Sadder, however, the poor soul who must twitch the foul thing out again. I know that soul. I call her by name. She has children and tired feet and bills and a blessed capacity for friendship. The custodian here at the Holiday Inn attends my church.

Sad cigarette. Sadder custodian . . .

Yet saddest of all, I believe, is the man who first *dropped* his butt here in a public place. This one is benighted. This one cannot—or will not—comprehend the consequences. Can't see that at the end of even his slightest act there always stands another, one whom he will scorn and trouble and cut, or else will love, by the act.

This fellow, this contemptuous flicker of cigarettes—however well he dresses, however solemnly he sits in his own church pew, however commanding, powerful, arrogant, smiling, self-satisfied, well-married, and prudent—can nevertheless *not* claim before God that he loves his neighbor as he loves himself, for he did not love my friend. He visited upon her a moment of moist, unnecessary misery.

This is the acid test. Do you love Christ Jesus? (Which question embraces this next one): Do you love the real manifestations of the Christ in the world around you? (Which question is the same as asking): Do you love the Body of Christ, the people whom Jesus loves? (Which question is made sharpest and purest in the following): *How* do you love the ones you do not meet, who cannot punish or reward you, blame or praise you, or in any way make the action anything more than the unvarnished (spontaneous) revelation of your natural self?

True love arises from the self alone, yours and mine, unqualified and free. Is it love when some threat drives me to it, or some payoff persuades me? A goodness given for a goodness gotten is a business transaction. No blame in that. No love either.

At the end of our least act, still affected by that act (for the world is shaped much more by the million little gestures than by the more glorious *res gestae* of human accomplishment) stands another. Always. And that human was made in the image of God.

———◆———

It is a radical truth that the Christ identifies much more with "the least of these" than with those of weight and repute in the world. "Radical," I say, because such a downward identification is a flat reversal of the way *we* choose to identify: upward, to those admirable, to those whose station flatters ours, whose power might empower us. We would be heroes. Jesus *is* the stranger. He *is*, in our common existence, the sick and the imprisoned.

How do we (as we will so often proclaim we do) love Jesus? With what attention and genuine love do we attend to the invisible people?

When I lean on the car horn loud and long, whose peace do I destroy? And how do I justify my anger now? Do I know the rules of the road better than the gentlewoman driving precisely the limit in front of me? And which of us is nearer the heart of Christ at this moment? And where is love?

When I neglect to signal a left-hand turn I neglect the driver behind me who might have gone forward in the right lane, had he known of my intention. But he has snuggled up to my back bumper, as has the driver behind him, and so *all* must now wait with me the oncoming traffic, drivers and drivers and Christ as well. (Or did I suppose that holiness rode in my vehicle alone?)

When I break the myriad little promises I make in a day (many of them made just to get *rid* of some persistent person) I break faith. I break my word. And though my word meant nothing to me, to my lessers it was the food of hope. Yes, and if in the littlest things I drop my bond and word thoughtlessly, like a butt in a urinal, in the greater, more "important" things that word will still be stinking of the urinal.

Laugh once at a "nigger" joke, and I've laughed at the skin of the Son of God, who chose to come enfleshed.

O man! When you speak of your wife as a fool, a ditz, a smiling second to your own great self, you shoot out the lip at your Savior. Do you not yet know that Christ both approaches you and tests you in your spouse? Woman, you cannot diminish his native interests without reducing his Creator (and yours) to the bozo you think your husband is.

If, by loud sighs and significant looks and angry gestures, you declare the old man ahead of you in the grocery line—tearing too slowly his food stamps from their packet—you have lost patience with Elisha, the bald-headed prophet of God.

Complain about the children in your neighborhood whose noise unnerves you—or about your own children, whose energy leaves you both angry and exhausted, febrile—and you have complained about those whom Jesus suffered into his presence, saying, "Of such is the kingdom of God."

And what of your father and mother when they descend into their dotage? (Teenagers often suspect that their parents have already entered the *Fuddy* stage, prelude to *Duddy,* by far the worse of the two.) If you despise them because of your vaster knowledge, your greater experience, your more contemporary ethic, your cooler view of life, you despise the instruments by which the Creator created *you.* Can you risk chopping the tree on which you are the fruit?

And surely you wouldn't assume that the only way to rate an employee is by her efficiency. Surely you would not cancel all the rest of this human by the stroke of your executive pen? But "cancel" means "kill" in affairs of the spirit.

Do you recognize that your mood at work is the very air your coworkers breathe? By which, in eight hours, in weeks and in the passage of years, they may thrive or else may suffocate?

———•◆•———

So, then:

Toss your fast-food wrappers on the highway.

Toss beer cans in the river.

Toss trash, the detritus of your burned-out desires; toss the very souls of those you use and lose; toss these wherever others do not see you, in the dark, in the night, in your unacknowledged solitude, away.

Toss a cigarette butt in a urinal, and you have made my dear friend miserable one more time, and she is the least of these, the sisters of Jesus.

And shall you rise in church tomorrow protesting your love for the Lord?

But we are more accurately revealed in the unconscious, habitual act than in acts we plan and for which we pay. In the former our truer nature dwells, and by it is made most manifest.

I am not writing of democracy. I'm not begging a political

equality of all individuals. I am begging rather the coming of the kingdom of heaven, whose citizens we are when we elevate the least to that same citizenship.

I am writing of love.

For at the end of *every* deed stands the Master—cleaning urinals.

Pallid Need

When you come to me biting your lip
Like linen and remorse, when you
Emerge from the darkness
And stand in my doorframe,
Beseeching ease
For the thing that brought you near
But fled you at the coming, when
You are a white Christ-candle here,
Scented of the sanctuaries,
Silent, robed and pale and still,
And waiting,
Oh, what word . . . shall I give you then?

To Joseph,
at His Confirmation

JOSEPH, MY SON, I AM PROUD OF YOU.

Tomorrow, before a smiling community of the faithful, the people who have hugged you half your life, you will confirm your own personal faith in Christ. A bold move, child, exciting and frightful all at once. You can't be the same person after it, nor can your relationships with others remain unchanged.

Child, with your confirmation tomorrow, you begin to be my child no longer.

You start in earnest the painful, private, personal, and finally triumphant toil of "growing up." You enter that which, when you will emerge from it, shall have made you an adult. The chrysalis, my Joseph, is something that prosaic souls call "adolescence," but something that demands of sons and daughters such heroic efforts that this father is moved by it now—now to tell you my pride in you.

You hardly know: to acknowledge yourself a child of God is to declare your independence from these earthly parents. You take your leave of Mom and me. And parts of you shall sink into yourself for no one's knowing but your own. Like creatures in a deep sea, when you are yourself that sea, certain thoughts and feelings shall never surface at your face; but you shall soon spread smiling over secret pain, and over some of your most blessed pleasures set a frown. In hiding, both Freedom and Anguish shall be born; and each shall feed the other till they grow into Leviathan and you're astonished that one so gentle, Joseph, could produce such monsters.

Oh, my son, what a task you begin! I'm thrilled to see it; I am terrified—both at once.

Well, it's a heady joy to watch you learn your legs, to see you engaged in the most consequential contest of all. No sport is more important or dramatic than this one, this *coming to be.* I groaned and clapped when you shot baskets successfully; how much louder I cheer you now at the graver game of *being!* Joseph, I am and I shall be your audience, and my spirit shall always applaud you—

But soon my pride shall seem so far away from you, and my cheering most distant (though it won't be any less), and you will feel so lonely, and you will have a right to that feeling, because you will be lonely indeed.

Ah, Joseph. Here is my fear at your chrysalid growing: that I can help you in this labor less and less until I help you not at all. I've no choice in the matter; and sometimes you will understand and demand that I let you alone (when independence will hurt me). Other times you will cry for a father to catch you, but I *will* let you alone (then independence will hurt you). No choice! This is the very index of the act. This *is* the act. Your "growing up" means needing to need me less, dear Joseph; and until you need me not at all, the labor remains unfinished, and my son remains merely my child.

It is this backing-off that scares me, this letting you into yourself. For neither of us knows what shape shall arise from private change. Will he, Heavenly God? Will my son succeed?

More than that, I choke, being all unable to share with you the storehouse of my own wisdom and experience, do choke, seeing you make the mistakes which I by a word could prevent.

And worst of all: I suffer with you the suffering of your loneliness. It's a one-way window. I can see, but in silence. You see only the mirror of yourself. I remember my own past pain, and I see its signs in you; yet the nature of your growing shall disallow my saying so or your believing it. You simply will not accept that I could know what you are going through. Irony, my son! For though your estimation of me shall be wrong, yet your action shall be right: You must struggle alone toward your majority.

How faint my cheering shall seem to you in those days, Joseph, how strengthless my support, how hollow my words of pride and love. That, precisely, is why I tell them to you now—right now, while you are at the slap-beginning of the process. I think that you still hear me.

And you'll feel such a rush of accomplishment tomorrow with your confirmation. I ride that rush with you. And you've the innocence still to see me here.

Oh, and there's one other reason why I cry my pride so loudly, now. . . .

———◆———

Too often the parents make absolutely nothing of their children's coming-of-age. They let it happen, as it were, by accident. Ho! They took more time over potty training than they take over training toward adulthood. They imply, then, that it is nothing, this "growing up"—or else that it is a distinct hazard in the household, a problem, a sin, a sickness, something that wants correcting. In consequence, the adolescent, unprepared, is shocked by the maelstrom he has entered. Next, he feels an abiding, unspoken guilt at the changes occurring in him. And when he most needs resources to fight this good fight, he least has them. Indeed, the fight seems anything but good and heroic when his voice breaks, her cramps come, but the family (neither parents nor society) has given no dignified name or place to these profound and exhausting efforts.

At the age of twelve I had to approach my father myself, myself to ask him whether he was proud of me. He'd neglected to mention it. It was a yearning question, and it stung that I had to ask it.

Listen to me, Joseph. Fold this letter. Put it away for reading again, when we've allowed each other our separation and you your quarantine. For this is the truth: I love you, son.

I am so proud of you.

Moses Swope

MOSES CORNELIUS 'TALITY SWOPE
had a problem.

———•◦•———

The problem wasn't with his eyes, his ears, or his nose.
These things worked very well on him.
When he saw a table, or a tiger, or a ghost, well,
he *saw* these things both big and clearly.
When he heard a bird, a train's whistle, or the devil's laughter, ho,
he truly *heard* these things, in his ear-hole, on the back of his neck.
When he smelled smoke or vinegar, popcorn or his mother's love,
     say, say,
he *smelled* them and his feelings turned in their breezes.
The problem wasn't with Moses' brains, either.
They could think so fast his head got hot.
Numbers went buzzing like bees through those brains, and words
     like butterflies,
and books and food and Bigfoot and heaven and hell and God,
a dizzy unstoppable storm.
He had good brains.

———•◦•———

And he had a good mouth, too.
Everything that he saw, or heard, or smelled, or thought about
he also talked about.

Three million words were in the mouth of Moses Swope.
That's more than ten, to be sure,
and his family would say, "Oh, Moses, be quiet."
Nope. The problem was not with his mouth.
The problem for Moses Cornelius Swope, well, well,
the problem was his FAITH.
Poor Moses *believed* most anything anyone told him.
And worse than that, dear Lord,
most everything Moses believed
came true!
Moses Cornelius Mortality Swope
had a very hard life.
"Don't eat candy! Don't suck sugar!" the dentist said.
"And most especially, stay away from chocolate, cookies, cakes
    and taffy apples!
Because otherwise all your teeth is gonna fall out!"
Well.
But on Hallowe'en, like any other kid, Moses went trick-or-
    treating,
and he popped a bubble gum into his mouth,
and before he remembered, he hammer-chewed that wad to
    death,
and then he remembered: "Oops."
But sure enough—that night
all of his teeth fell out.

————◆————

"Now, don't be playing with them white kids, Mose," said his
    brother, Junior,
and he shook a hair-pick in the face of Moses and he nodded.
"Because one day one of them's gone to touch you.
And look here. Just one touch from a white boy's skin,
and *your* skin gone turn white as leprosy. How 'bout that?"
Well.

Moses, he called up his white friends on the telephone
and told them to leave him alone. "Just lea' me alone!" he said.
Moses, he went to school with his head down,
and he sat in his desk with his head down: he said,
"Don' look lef' and don' look right. Be tiny, Mose."
Because he was a-scared of leprosy.
So here came the teacher, and what did she say?
She said, "Moses, are you sick?" He shook his head.
She said, "Moses, are you sad?" He put out his lip.
So here come the teacher, and what did she do?
She put her hand on Moses' shoulder, Lord, Lord!
And sure enough—that shoulder
got leprosy, turned white as the teacher's hand.
Moses, why didn't you listen?

———— ◆ ————

Moses' sister, she frowned when she pulled the sheets from
     Moses' bed.
Serious frowning, smoky-o face, no man in the lady's life to
     speak of,
but laundry forever and ever.
"Boy!" she said, and why were the tears in her eyes?
"You, boy!" Because Moses had done something terrible?
"You pee in this bed just one more time," she said,
"and you know what God's gone do to you?"

———— ◆ ————

Moses Cornelius 'Tality Swope shook his head.
"He gone to cut your trigger off, and you ain't never gone shoot
     again!"
Well.
Moses had but one trigger, willful altogether!
He went to bed with everything tight,

and he prayed to God for no pee-water in his belly.
"Spit a lot, ole Mose! Go spit it out!"
And this is the way he went to sleep;
but he peed in bed,
and sure enough—God
cut his trigger off.
Ain't gone to shoot no more, poor Moses. No more shots in you.
Moses Cornelius 'Tality Swope,
no teeth, no trigger, no friends on the street,
and leprosy down from his shoulder, well.
It's what you get when you don't listen, Lord.
It's what you get when you be bad.

———◆———

But the harmfulest thing of all was the word of his Mama to
　　him,
and the hurtfulest thing of all, on account of *she* figured to suffer
for the trouble poor Moses he caused in the world,
and she was so weary so most of the time,
cause who was there worked in the family but her,
cause where was her husband? Where was his father?
Got none. No, never did.
"Can't stand it no more, my Moses," she said,
wheezing and leaning against his doorway.
"If you don' be good, my Moses Corn," she said, "it's goin' to kill
　　me,
child.
If you don' pick up behind, if you don' be home on time, if you
　　don'
come and run and mind, your Mama is just goin' to die.
You'll be the death of me yet, Moses Corn."
Well.
Who was softer than Moses after that?

Who done the dishes more carefuller than him?
Who swept the kitchen, carried trash, and tucked his Mama into
    bed?
And who broke his window with the handle of the broom?
It was a very loud crash. The gates of heaven broke.
His Mama lumbered into his room. She looked at the glass.
She opened her mouth. She raised her hands.
And Moses wished that he would get a switching,
but sure enough—
she died instead.
Moses, he started to cry.
Moses, he patted his hands together, because, why didn't
    somebody switch him?
Moses, he put one foot in front of the other,
which was the same as walking,
and out of the house he went,
and this is what Moses Cornelius Mortality Swope did:
he ran away.
He ran away as fast as he could go,
little Black boy, turning white.
So he took whatever sidewalk was in front of him, Jesus, Jesus.
He ran so blind, cause he was running nowhere, don't you know?
Was *from* that he was running: huff a block, puff another;
From the house
and *from* his Mama on the floor
and *from* his thousand miserablenesses
and *from* his own rotten, run-down *self.*
And maybe he would find a hole, black to the bottom of the
    earth,
and maybe he could fall into it—
"Moses, you a curse on yourself!
Moses, you a murderer!"
Then, where did the boy run out of his breath?
Under the bridge.

A thousand cars going over; life going over the river; rumbling
  talk
of the city, mindless of Moses down by brown water and
  thinking
that when he got his breath again, he would go into the river and
  float away
forever.
Who cared if somebody peed in the river?
A voice said, "I care."
Instantly, Moses pretended that he didn't hear any voice.
There was no one else under the bridge, nowhere around.
Therefore, if he heard a voice, that meant that he was crazy.
The voice said, "Oh, I am *so* holy. And I'm *so* busy runnin' this
  bad old world.
But you know what, Moses my man? I got the time anyway, and
  I care."
Moses rolled his eyes to the water, cause that's where this voice
seemed to come from.
He whispered, "I cain't see you."
The voice began to laugh. "On account of, I'm a spirit, ho-ho!
  Ho-ho!"
The voice had a coughing fit, right over the water.
Moses said, "I'm crazy."
"Insane, my man, completely insane," said the voice. "Lookee
  here: Do you want to see me?"
Moses said, "I want to die."
"All in good time," said the voice. "Moses," it said, "you got a
  mouth?"
"Yes," said Moses, and the cars and trucks rumbled over his
  head.
"Good. And you got words in your mouth?"
"Three million," said Moses.
"Good. Then say this: say, you got skin, old man.
And when you say it, listen to your miserable self.

And when you listen, believe it."

Moses Cornelius Mortality Swope, the boy beneath the city
bridge, whispered, "You got skin, old man."

And there before his eyes appeared a skinny old man, black as
the Bible, bent and naked, except for a loin cloth, walking,
walking on the flowing river in order to stay in front of
Moses.

And look-ee here: the old man was grinning.

"See what you can do?" laughed the old man. "Here I am! Oh,
you been a sucker, boy, for the words of every con around
you. Hoo, you been crazy, all right. Didn't you never think
that maybe *you* could do some of the talking and maybe
believe in some of the things *you* said?"

"But my Mama is dead," said Moses Corn.

"Now, that's what *she* said," said the old man. "What do *you* say?"

Poor Moses only stared at the trudging individual. "Who are
you?" he said.

The old man picked up one foot and hopped on the other.

He showed his foot to Moses. The bottom looked wood-stained
and shiny.

Moses saw a hole in it.

"Does that tell you something?" asked the old man.

"You was hurt?" said Moses. "Did I hurt you?"

"Hallelujah, child! You've a slow wit but improvin'. I'm Jesus,
don't you know. This here's from my crucifixion, a left-over
scar. Did you ever hear tell of anyone else who walked on
the water?"

"No."

"Well, amen, then."

"But, is Jesus so old?"

"Sucker, you done *made* me old! Done put me to pasture with
your foolishness. Now, look-ee here: I heal bodies, right?
And I forgive the sins of the children, right? It's been my
business, lo, some goin' on two thousand years. But did you

ever *say* so to believe it? Where's your amen? And I'm the
one that goes raisin' folks from the dead. Can I have an
amen to that, too?"

Moses said, "Amen."

"Now you talkin', child! And be you listenin' to your miserable
self?

And can you believe the thing you say?"

Moses said, "But I thought Jesus, he was young."

"Thought?" said the old man.

"Think," said Moses.

"*What* you think, boy? Say it!"

"I think that Jesus, he was young."

"Was?" cried the old man at the top of his lungs. "Was, boy?"

"Is," said Moses.

"*Done!*" cried the old man, and he clapped his hands,
and where the skin hit skin a lighting bolt went out,
and thunder ripped the river,
and Moses covered his face with his hands and trembled,
and when the thunder rolled away, he peeped out again,
and there was the man, still walking on the river,
still grinning with all of his teeth stuck out,
still wearing nothing but a loincloth, and black as the Bible,
    still—
but young, young, the most handsome, purebred stallion of a
    man
that Moses Swope had ever seen.

Oh, he held his head so high, and the pads of his feet flashed
    pink
when he slooped them from the water, and his hands was *dancing!*

"Jesus?" Moses said.

"Amen to your miserable self," said Jesus. "Amen to your mouth,
    Boy," he laughed. "Amen, amen to my own mos' holy name,
    ho, ho!"

Moses stood up on the river bank and began to grin. "Jesus?"

"Now, don't you be trying the water-walkin' trick," said Jesus. "I
    be catchin' one too many no-counts from the drink. Go on;
    stay put. The way it is, is: I come to you." And he walked to
    shore.
"Jesus!" cried Moses Cornelius.
And when the muscular Black man stepped ashore, the boy
    threw his arms around him and laid his face against his chest
    and began to cry so hard that the big man stroked his head.
"Shoosh. Shoosh. You see what you done, don't you?" Jesus
    whispered. "Done thought it, done said it, done believed it,
    done *done* it. Here I am, boy, young and so pretty to knock
    your eyes out. But I was always here. So what you listen to
    suckers for? What for you give them your beliefs? Don't you
    know, Moses my man, oh brother, brother Moses—I care for
    you?"
"Jesus?"
"What?"
"O Jesus, my Mama is dead," said Moses, his head so down in
    misery that he seemed a brown puddle.
But the big man grabbed that boy by both his ears, like a jug, and
    lifted him off the ground, stared at him eye to eye. "Dead.
    Hum. So she says. And what else? Come on, boy—what
    else?"
"Well," said Moses floating, "and I ain' got no teeth."
Toothless. Hum. So the dentis' say. And what else?"
"Leprosy?"
"Hum. A damn ignernt disease—so the brother say. And what
    else?"
"Well," said Moses, hanging like a sack, embarrassed.
"Well?" said Jesus.
"Well, and I ain't got no—trigger," said Moses.
"Triggerless! Ho, ho! Triggerless—so the sister say. Oh, ho, ho,
    ho!"

Jesus took to laughing hard. Horse-laughing. Laughing, he laid
the boy aground.

Laughing, slapping his knee with one hand, he scratched in his
loincloth with the other. Laughing till the tears ran down his
cheeks, he pulled out a yellow grain between two fingers.
"Oh, little brother, *triggerless!* Them things do grow, don't you
know? Look-ee here," he said, and he kneeled down next to
the boy, and he skewed Moses' lips apart, and he planted the
grain in Moses' gum. "I'll help you with the teeth. This
here's a mustard seed, don't you know, better than teeth.
You talk with it, you talk with faith. *Faith,* man!"

He slapped the boy on his shoulder.

Moses coughed.

"Now," said Jesus, "it's my profession to be raisin' people from
the dead. And I don't shirk, and I don't shuffle. But what I
do, I delegate. I send folks to be doin' for me. Moses,
brother, go for me. Go talk to your Mama. Go tell her the
truth. You big enough, now. Shoot," said Jesus, "you a *man,*
now!"

The big man, sleek as a horse, walked out on the water again,
and sat down,
and floated away.

He bowed his head, and his shoulders were shaking,
because he was laughing.

And the last word that Moses heard before the bend in the river
was

"Hee, hee! Triggerless! Hee, hee, hee!"

Well, when he heard the cars and the trucks on the bridge again,
the first thing that Moses Cornelius 'Tality Swope did
was to say,

"In my pants," and he giggled a little like the Lord,
"is a proud and pretty trigger."

And he peeped into his pants,

and there it was, a fine fresh trigger, well, amen!
And then he laughed *exactly* like the Lord: Ho hos all over the
 place.

———◆———

The second thing that he did,
was to say, "Moses Corn, you can touch yourself as well as
 anyone can!"
And he said, "Skin to skin. Mine to me!"
And he tore his shirt, and he took the rich back of his hand,
and Moses touched Moses, and Moses was Moses again.
Amen!
The leprosy peeled right off.
Amen, amen to that!

———◆———

But the third thing that he did
was the most important thing of all.
He ran home, and he burst into the house: "Mama? Mama?"
He found his Mama lying on the floor, huge as a mountain.
And he said into her little ear,
"Oh, Mama, this is the truth: I love you!
And Jesus said, you ain't dead, really."
He wet his lips, and onto her shiny cheek he put a fat and drippy
 kiss,
and into her hair went a tear,
and he said, "No, Mama, I ain't the death of you.
What I am is, I'm the life of you on account of how much I love
 you.
Oh, Mama, Mama."
Moses Cornelius 'Tality Swope hugged his poor Mama,
until she sat up, and rolled down her stockings to the ankle,
and sighed, and patted his cheek,

and went to make him dinner.

And Jesus said, from the air around him, "Well, finally, sucker.
   And amen to that!"

And his Mama called, "Boy, you watch your mouth."

And Moses burst out laughing.

To Matthew,
at His Confirmation

MATTHEW, MY SON, how far we have come together. How much we have raised each other. How good it has been.

I first saw you in a crib—thick neck, enormous eyes, compact brown energy, fine amber hair, and I thought, "Can I love this one?"

You were three months old then. You kept your body stiff as a stick the whole way home from Indianapolis. Mom felt she had firewood on her lap. You didn't sleep well that night, stranger in a strange bed; nor did you sleep easily the year thereafter. You were a wakeful babe in every way. And I thought, "Can I love this one?"

Well, I'd been a father one bare year; Joseph was the first, but you were the first we adopted, so I had little experience at the job and no knowledge at all whether a parent loves the ready-made child as much as the child that comes from his own loins. I wondered if we missed some mysterious ingredient since you arrived of a mental decision and not of the physical love of your parents; and you were brown and I was white. Where was the love to come from?

Here is the miracle: my love for you came out of you! You came with printed directions. You trained me.

———◆———

At first it was a foolish love, aggressive, fierce, protective. When we carried you to the grocery stores, we gathered the stares of the people. Our family was a riddle they couldn't solve. My ears would burn at their ill restraint; I'd grab you to my heart and stare back to shame their eyes. My face said, "*Mine!* He's mine, you little minds!" And so you were.

There was a neighbor, in those early days, who said that you couldn't play with her daughter. She'd seen the two of you holding hands, and she said, "Black and white don't marry." Nip it, I suppose, in the bud: you were four years old. I sat in that woman's kitchen and in a low, choked voice declared you were my son and she should think of me precisely as she thought of you. Curiously, she acted as though she and I were the buddies and you the odd boy out, since she and I were white together. But to me her kitchen was alien territory, and she the foreigner, and I despised her stainless steel complacency; I hated her hatreds, and I hugged you hard when I went home again, but you didn't understand that nor the burning love begun in me, half angry, half apologetic. You took my love for granted. You were the wiser, and you trained me.

Baby boy, you gentled that love.

And you expanded it.

Hungry, hungry for all experience, you attempted anything life offered, and my heart went with you. In you I knew a wild existence; without you I was too shy to try it.

One hour after you had learned to ride a bike, you built a ramp at the bottom of a hill: Evel Knievel! Down that hill you hurtled. You hit the ramp at top speed. The bike stopped cold, and you flew over it. When I held you, then, I said, "Don't cry, my adopted son." In dear moments I used the word "adopted" so that it would seem a good word to you and a good thing.

In winter you climbed the ice, stranding yourself on the overflow waters of Pigeon Creek. Oh, wailing boy on a rocky ice island!

Like the "Six Millions Dollar Man" (your hero before Terry Bradshaw, Franco Harris, and the Steelers) you tried to open the bedroom door with your foot. "Ha-YAAA!" I heard through the house, and then a splintering crash, and the pictures on the walls slid sideways. I ran. I found the door still shut, but a foot stuck through it; and when I pulled the door open, a boy dragged out on his back, smiling. Such committed loyalties you made, O my adopted son. To the ones you honored, you gave yourself completely, totally.

You trained me.

But the second miracle and the second source of my love for you was marvelous, holy, and indestructible, the greatest of them all. I came to understand, through the years, that it is in the very image of adoption, and thus divine, that God participates—

———•◆•———

The last time ever that I spanked you, you barked your pain and stiffened on my knees and pierced me to the heart: I had hurt you. I sat you down in a chair and left the room. I went out, and I myself burst into tears.

It was a terrible, thwarted thing—for me to cry.

I said, "God, how can I know if I'm a good father to this child?" I said, "God, please, *you* be father for him—"

And quietly I understood: in fact, God *is* your father, and a better one than I. But God and I both became your fathers in exactly the same way. Matthew, God also adopted you! You were not born his son, either. It was something that he chose to do for you. But his adoption contains a love unspeakably sweet and powerful, far beyond my poor, fumbling efforts. I'm in extraordinary company! Therefore, I went back into the room and held you, at peace in this wisdom that he is the source; and you, by the grace of God, you held me back.

Oh, my adopted son! My love for you and my fatherhood both I hide completely in the remarkable love and fatherhood of

God for you. *There* is where this wonder comes from. *He* patterns and empowers it. For a little while he allows me to experience the self-same joy that he has loving you. For a little while he lets me be your father—just like him.

But tomorrow, Sunday, he begins to take over; the real is revealed, and I diminish. You are growing up.

Tomorrow, before the entire congregation, you will proclaim your personal faith in him, because it is your confirmation day. You will say "Yes!" out loud and consciously: "Yes!" to confirm the adoption he began. "Yes! I am a child of God!"

How glad I will be to hear that, because my love is strong, but my strength weaker than my love, and I do sin, but then the Holy Father will be holding you, and nothing, nothing can pluck you from those hands. How relieved I will be to hear that.

———◆———

Who says adoption makes a lesser relationship than blood or the will of the flesh? Let him contend with the Almighty! And let him be ashamed.

Can I love this one—brown thunder after my white lightning?

Ah, my son, my son! By God, I do. By God, I shall love you forever.

The Ashes of Wednesday,
for Thieves and for
Preachers Alike

I THINK I THOUGHT I had solid reasons for moral superiority. I was not a thief. I was not an extortioner. I was no citizen of the night, but of the light. A pastor, in fact, was I—responsible for this church and its building, both: *this* building (slap the brick!) This very one.

———•◆•———

It was Tuesday night late February. Lucian Snaden and I were standing alone on the east side of the church, watching for his mother and her car.

Earlier I'd been teaching my adult confirmation class a lesson in the Christian faith ... until the thunderstorm outside had finally grown too violent for continuing. The interior lights flashed. I went up the stairs and stuck my head into the night: under hard swipes of rain, the streets were already a rashy flood, the sidewalks submerged. In a hubbub, then, the folks of my class covered themselves and fled to their cars. Lucian and I pushed several of these to higher ground before they would turn the ignition key. We lent our backs to the beautiful Rita Cooksey, bearing her dry-shod to her vehicle. He telephoned his mother to say that the class was over early, could she come. And then we two were left alone, outside, under a little shingle of roof, watching. The wind had not abated, but the rainfall had turned to mist and we were already wet. We'd see his mother at a distance. He would run to keep her from the nearer inundations.

The entire Grace Church facility sat relatively high on the corner of Eliot and Gum, both the sanctuary and the parish house immediately west of it. That neat, small house had once been a parsonage and then a rental. A year ago we'd moved our offices into it, gaining a little, losing a little in the exchange. We surely were glad of the extra space; it represented the healthy growth of this congregation. But we gave up a little income; and, what was the heavier loss, the house itself was often empty and vulnerable, therefore, to burglary. This was the inner city. Drugs and guns and various dangers strolled the midnight streets. Twice in the last three months we'd had to repair and replace windows and equipment stolen.

"Coming back tomorrow evening?" I asked Lucian in order to pass the time. "Seven o'clock?"

The wind cut round the corners like an army, but it was from the west and we stood up against the eastern doors.

Lucian didn't answer immediately. In this young man never lived the itch of haste. He studied on a question as though it were a vocation—and sometimes found no proper answer at all.

Lightning scored the heavens, igniting the thousand droplets in Lucian's hair like a sky of stars; then it dropped a BOOM! of terrible weight. My skin tightened.

"Ash Wednesday," I said. "It's a good way to start observing Lent—by worshipping, I mean. Tomorrow evening. A person can confess his sins, all his sins, and Jesus forgives him. I'll touch the tip of my finger to ashes and mark your forehead with a cross, and—"

CRASH! I paused a moment, listening.

Glass. Some sort of glass had shattered on the far side of the church building.

"Lucian, just a minute." I raised an index finger, then stepped down from the porch, going to investigate what kind of damage the wind had done. Into its spitting face, I circled the northern side of the building, turning left and coming up to the narrow passage between the church and the parish house.

Lightning stuttered above, suddenly illuminating the dark corridor—and there; slickly, suddenly outlined; crouching against the house-wall; actually *reaching* his arm through a broken window into *my* office: was a thief! Was an idiot robber!

"Look at me!" I bellowed.

Our third break-in, and I went straight to rage.

But it was the crass stupidity of the act that split my brain with the rage. The lights in the church were *lit!* The pastor was *here!*

"Let me see your face," I thundered. "I will remember you!"

The thief started at the sound of my voice, snatched back his arm, turned for a frozen instant toward me, then whirled away and clattered south, out the chute between the buildings.

His image stuck to the back of my sight: thin, young, gaunt, terrified. It sent a perfect thrill of fury down my legs and I, too, ran.

He went slipping down the southern lawn. I did not slip. I was a lion of rectitude, a deer of marvelous grace!

Lightning flashed. The thief was casting a backward glance. He blinked rapidly. His wiry legs wound together like a braid.

BOOM! commanded the thunder, and the fellow careened head-forward into the floods at the banks of Gum Street.

He squirmed round to his back—even as I leaped and flew and fell bodily upon him. Lightning flashed: huge were his eyes, and white, and wild with an uncomprehending horror.

Oh, what power this granted me! I put my left hand flat against his chest, pushed my torso upward from the waist.

BOOM! said the thunder. And again, BOOM!

Raising my right arm high to the sky, I kept my furious gaze upon the thief and roared out above him: "THE THUNDER IS FOR YOU, FOOL! THE VOICE OF GOD! THE VOICE OF THE LORD IS SAYING *LEAVE THIS CHURCH AND NEVER, NEVER COME BACK!*"

So said I without a moment's thought or preparation. It poured with high drama from my mouth, from my blazing mind, from my heart.

And I felt wonderful. At one was I, attuned to the universe!

When the thief, gone skeletal, wriggled and twisted and shot like springs from beneath my body and over the waters, I was not disappointed. I had, I thought, accomplished the thing of primary importance: protected our stuff.

Seldom in my life have I had such opportunity (and such immediate ability) to experience winged victory in my own mortal chest.

I returned to Lucian smiling.

But of course, in the aftermath of storm he could not see the smile nor note the triumph in my eyes.

So I said, "Guess what I just did?"

And he, peering steadfastly up Eliot, said, "What?"

And I: "I caught a thief. I drove a thief away."

Then, replaying the scene within me, I added: "Young fellow. Pitiful idiot. I said that God said never to come to this church again!"

Lucian Snaden stopped looking for his mother's car. I felt his dark face angle down toward mine. And the lightning flashed, and I saw the dreadful knot of a frown on Lucian's brow.

He said slowly, in the form of a question, "Told someone? Not and never? To come to church? Pastor?"

Dutifully, the thunder said, "Boom."

And Lucian concluded the question of his confusion: "But you asked me. To come tomorrow. Evening at seven. Didn't you?"

———•———

"*Memento, homo,*" say the pastors to every penitent that comes and kneels in the chancel. There is a continuous line of the faithful rising in their pews, processing forward, and another line returning to their pews, darkly marked.

This is the Wednesday of the Ashes.

"*Memento,*" the pastors say, pressing their fingers into bowls of soft ash, then striking two dusty lines, one across the other, on the brows of the men and women still kneeling here: "*Memento, homo, quia pulvus es, et in pulverem reverteris.*"

———◆———

Listen, children: during the worship service this Ash Wednesday, before I touch your foreheads with the signs of our Lord's death and of his forgiveness, let someone touch mine first.

Before I murmur the terrible words to anyone else, let them be murmured in my ear and deeply to my heart: "Remember, mortal: dust you are, and to dust you shall return."

Let me be so persuaded of my own mortality that never again do I seek righteousness or life within me. Such arrogant presumptions make of preachers and leaders the greater thieves after all; for they would keep as theirs the grace God gives to *every* other.

Who among us will claim a moral superiority? Who can? Who is able, or else has the right?

There is but one in all this universe superior to sin, in whom is life and immortality; and he falls down from heaven like light upon the places here below. His is a thunder of mercy, and his love is a storm.

To Mary,
at Her Confirmation

MARY, GOD LOVED YOU FIRST. Please, dear child, remember that.

Before Mom and I fell in love with you (and we were two of the first to fall in love with you), God loved you.

Before we even met your chunky self or knew what kind of child was living behind those gazing-blue eyes, hungry-blue, curious and laughing-blue eyes; before you grabbed my finger the first time; before you came somewhat shocked and blood-streaked into the air of this world; before you bulked in Mom's womb, lying on the inside, protected; before you wriggled secretly in the deepest regions of her being, when none on the earth knew that there *was* a you about to share the earth with us—in that most solitary time when you had just come to be, but had no name yet, no face, no human shape or thoughts or dreams or fears or fancies; when, like the primal cell, you had but being only and all the rest was possibility, then, Mary, even *then* God loved you.

Yes, yes, it is impossible for anyone to remember back that far. I know it. But that is precisely my point: God remembers. God it was who formed your inward parts, who knit you together in your mother's womb. Your frame was not hidden from him when you were being made in secret, intricately wrought in the depths of the earth.

———◆———

Before we knew you, God knew and loved you very well.

I tell you that, Mary, in order to prepare you for the difficulty buried in your confirmation day tomorrow, Sunday, May 26, 1985.

But you have a beautiful dress to wear, don't you? And high anticipations for the day. Laughter turns your round face pink! On your own legs, in your own voice, according to your own sole faith, you will declare before the people that Jesus is your Lord and your Savior. Neither Mom nor I will say this for you. *You* will say: "I believe. This is who I am now: I believe in Jesus Christ, who suffered and was crucified and died and was buried and on the third day rose from the dead, and all this, all this for me."

I will listen to you, and I will draw my breath in a sweet sharp pain, seeing that my daughter has grown up. With your confession you become an independent person. In spirit, an adult. And so it should be: you have been yearning for your independence many long years now, flying up the stairs and into your bedroom, wailing: "Why can't I do the things *I* want to do?" You have chalked a purple makeup on your face, designing that face as *you* imagine it, creating your very self, then flying up the stairs when I told you to wash it off. "Nobody understands me! I am *suffocating* in this house!"

You have flown high-minded, Mary, reaching for such a supernal justice that my plain pragmatism seemed to you as heavy as lead, cold and reprehensible.

Joy in you lifts your very heart to the heavens. Joy in you is a kestrel's flight, straight into the wind, the perpetual dash.

It is, isn't it, your nature to fly?

And there is the difficulty, hidden to you but visible and inevitable to me.

For one day in your soaring freedom you will chance to look down, and suddenly you will see how high you've gone, then various realities will seize your soul: how lonely is such flight! How far the fall! How hard and heartless the rocky world below.

In that day you will cry out for me, but I won't be there as I have been.

"Daddy!" you'll wail. "Catch me! I'm falling!"

And the fact that I do not answer will horrify you. It will seem such a betrayal of our love, though it was *you* who took flight, remember? And it was right when you did. Remember?

Well, Mary, in that terrible moment of reversals, remember this too: God loved you first. God has always loved you. God formed you in his love, and by his love sustains you still.

My love had a beginning. Mine is human, and though I love you to the end, that can last no longer than *my* end, my limits and my death. Moreover, to me you cannot be forever a child.

But to God you are forever a child. And wherever his child chooses to go, there is the Holy Parent beside you. As early as God's love preceded Mom's and mine, even so long shall his love last after ours.

Therefore, however frightful the fall may seem, cry out for God. As once you threw yourself with dramatic abandon upon your bed, so throw yourself still on the bosom of Jesus.

———◆———

I have a photograph of, my Mary, in which you are sitting and reading a book. Your head is bent; your hair hangs down on one side, lower than your neck, but breaking at your ear; you are soft in a striped and flannel nightgown; and you are deep in meditations. It is as though your spirit has flown out of you, into the story that had already stolen your eyes. You are beautiful—and you are gone, both at once.

When I look at this photograph, my heart is troubled.

I think, "Where has the gentle child gone?" Not for you, now, Mary, but for me is my fear: "I don't even know the direction she's taken. I don't know what world she has gone to inhabit." And—precisely because it *is* a photograph, fixed and impenetrable—I feel somewhat abandoned. "The world she knows, it is not mine."

This picture of you instructs me *too* of the future, when you shall fly where I can't follow. When my love for you can no longer flood you, feed you, be so fully expressed to you.

But then I, like you, will take dear comfort in this, that God loved you first. I am earthbound, indeed; but the Spirit of God is not. And in my loneliness I shall say, "But my Mary is not alone."

For wither can you go, my darling, from the Spirit of the Lord? If you mount to the heavens on a giddy, deceitful joy, God is there. If you make your bed in the pit of the dead, God is there. If you take the wings of the morning and dwell in the uttermost parts of the sea, even there God's hand shall lead you, his own right hand shall cover you.

Tomorrow, Mary, I give you to God.

When you sturdily confirm the covenant you have with God, then you leave me. And then I let you go. These are two distinct acts, performed (when it is well) by the child and the parent as one and at once. Yours is a boldness, mine an obedience. Yours loves the future toward which you rush; mine permits that future, losing you for love of you. These are the twin gestures of growth and letting go: when they happen together, freely, willingly, they are as divine as Noah's dove, the third time he sent her forth and she did not return.

But these gestures would be neither divine nor good nor possible if you left God as well, Mary, or if God should choose to let you go. In fact, at leaving me you go *to* God. And he will not let you go. Not ever. No, never! He soars with you. He wraps you in the rainbow—and I am content, for you are safe, my daughter. He who loved you first shall love you always, always. Always. . . .

For My Brother Gregory on the Occasion of His Marriage to Liza Lachica

ALL THE BLESSINGS OF GOD, my brother, upon this thing that you and Liza are beginning! He took time and care and mercy to create no other human relationship but this one. That relationship between parent and child; or that between ruler and ruled, between neighbor and neighbor, brother and sister, or that between the colaborers—none of these received the same creative attention as the one you and Liza are now compacting with each other. Thus the depth of his concern for it: it is holy, Greg. It is different. It bears a divinity. The consequences of its rightness or its wrongness are more profound, more blessed or hurtful to you and others than the consequences of any other relationship between people, for it shall shape you and Liza and your children in all these others.

God's blessings, brother, on your marriage.

———◆———

Your heart convinced you of this decision. You love Liza. Her heart agreed. She loves you. It is an exquisite meeting between the two, and a sweet harmony greatly to be wondered at, for this conjunction more nearly strikes the image of God than either one of you alone.

But please permit me, Greg, to caution you.

Love may begin a marriage; but love does not make a marriage. You will ride a wild sea, if you think you can build your marriage upon your love. In fact, it is exactly the other way around: your love, eventually, shall be built upon your marriage.

Well, look. If marriage depends upon love, what will you do tomorrow when you discover that Liza's feet stink? Or when you discover that she's got a stubborn streak well hidden during courtship, which, behind stiff lips, is as silent as the tomb and puts her a thousand miles away from you, even when you're sitting across the table from one another? Or that she pouts? What will you do with such post-connubial, bedroom revelations?

I tell you, these cold shocks can freeze a love as fast as the northern wind. And then, lacking love, what will you do? Divorce her? (I don't mean merely legally, since divorce can be written on thin lips and in the flashing eye as well as on a legal document.) Shall marriage die when love does—expire on the closer battlefields of bathroom, kitchen, and the bunker bedroom? And when love warms up again, what? Are you married again? No, Greg. Such sea-changes would cause a confusion from which the both of you would finally seek release.

But marriage should be itself the solid thing to hold an evanescent love. Marriage is the arena in which love comes, acts, goes, and comes again. Marriage is the house to hold your unpredictable hearts. Marriage, ultimately, is the soil from which a finer love—a sacrificial love—may spring and grow. Marriage itself, by your conscious decisions, is the thing, the bedrock, the reality, that which is to be trusted. And love is the blessing on that marriage.

You do not love in order to have a marriage. You have a marriage in order, sometimes, to love.

———— • ————

Well, after that fusillade of opinion, dear younger brother, I'd better define the thing I'm calling "marriage" in better terms than metaphor, right? Fine.

Marriage is a common act between you, common for two reasons:

1. You both perform, independently, the self-same act. You promise your lives to one another, wholly, daily, and without end. Publicly you pronounce oaths (this though neither of you knows exactly what you're getting in the bargain; that is discovered only in the doing).

2. You both trust absolutely the promise of the other (even though the oath has not yet truly been tested, since trust is commitment without all the facts to hand). Marriage, to be brief, is the vows of two, faithfully given, faithfully received, and binding despite both time and ignorance.

Neither whim, nor life-circumstances, nor stinky feet, nor even the sins of either of you dissolves these vows. Nor love lost. For what in fact does a vow have to do with any of these things? (Which is, of course, the whole point of a vow, something immutable in mutability!) Since death alone cancels the votary, death alone cancels the vow.

I suppose that seems almost cruelly rigid to you, Greg? It is. Houses are built of a wise rigidity. And I recognize that if this were all, it might squeeze your changing, spontaneous selves to death. For how, says all the world, can one make an everlasting promise in ignorance? And what of the hurts and the mistakes that each of you shall surely deliver the other?

Well, but there is one other essential element to your marriage that makes the house-building possible (which makes the house a living thing, not stone alone), and that shall permit you not to break under the sinful hurts, but rather to heal and grow the stronger. This is the element that ultimately plants the highest form of love in the soil of marriage. This, my dear brother Greg, you cannot do without:

Forgiveness.

That you can forgive one another the sins which shall surely come is the growth and flexibility of a rigid house. It is the one single thing in all the world that saves marriages and fosters their maturity. Even the much-vaunted "communication" is only a tool, good in a good hand, bad in a bad. Communication often magnifies a sin. Forgiveness alone puts that sin away.

You smile. You say, "Oh, we knew that. People sin, people forgive, and people go on."

I smile. I say, "That's only the game-plan, but half of the truth, and none of the power. Let me finish your sentences for you. People sin—infinitely. People forgive—only finitely. And given that crippled equation, people cannot go on."

Now hear me, Greg. You can forgive Liza a little. Love's a firecracker, all right; but it is not the sun. You alone cannot forgive her forever, nor ever to the measure that she can sin against you. You will say, with all of the men of the world, "There's a limit!" or "I can take only so much and no more!" or "I'm tired, Liza, worn out. I quit." And she would say the same to you. Humans die, don't you know. Human resource is sadly quantifiable. And human relationships are no greater than the souls that feed them—may die as well.

Your marriage, then, would be doomed to a limited existence, either in its time or in its depth—except for this: that Jesus Christ forgives forever and infinitely!

I'll say it straight. Without his resource to alpha-and-omega it, I could with my small mind span your marriage from its beginning to its end. It is Christ whom you must, each of you, draw upon. You make the marriage; but he doth heal and nourish it. His is forgiveness without end.

Therefore, Greg, for Liza's sake, acknowledge most earnestly that for your infinite sin against Christ, Christ pours infinite forgiveness into you. (It must, first, be personal and Liza-less, this act.) That establishes the relationship of faith and makes, in you, a bottomless well of the Lord Jesus. *Then* turn to Liza. Christ's forgiving you, Greg, enables you, Greg, to forgive Liza in the same measure as she needs forgiveness. And his forgiving of Liza, Greg, will make his infinitely merciful face to appear in *her* face for you. You will look at Liza, and behold! You will see Jesus. And then—then, for God's sake—will you be able to believe in *her* word of forgiveness for *your* measureless sin.

Do you see, dear brother? Christ, the life of your vows, is himself the life of your marriage!

So build a house, Greg and Liza. Of the vows and of forgiveness, build a mansion for your hearts.

Fights Unfought,
Forgiveness Forgone

BEHOLD THE STIFF-NECKED, the hard-hearted, the dummy!

Observe the camel, blind to one of the most useful gifts of the Lord God—which is that he arranges opportunities for confession and forgiveness between warring individuals, that they might smile and love again. He does so squarely in their day's experience. Yet note well how fierce can be the pride of this blockhead, and learn from him: it's a damnfool practice, to ignore the armistice that God keeps staging.

Behold me, when first my wife and I were married.

Lo! I am the dummy.

———◆———

We used to fight, Thanne and I.

Well, it was always a "sort-of" fight, on account of it was all one-sided. I did the talking. She did the not-talking. And then what she did was, she would cry.

I would say, "Thanne, what's the matter?" Real sympathy in my voice, you understand. And caring and gentleness in abundance, and great-hearted love. Dog-eyed solicitation: "Oh, Thanne, what is the matter?"

And she would only cry.

So then, I had my second stratagem. So then, I would sigh loudly in order to indicate that I have troubles, too, not the least of which is an uncommunicative wife—and how are we going to solve anything if we don't *say* anything? (I was skilled at the sophisticated sigh.) And I would ask again, allowing just a tad of aggravation to bite my voice, "What *is* the matter, Thanne?"

For all of which I might receive a head shake from the woman—and crying.

Now, silence is a saw-toothed tool of the devil. It's also excellent for self-righteous fighting, because it permits the other to imagine the myriad sins he must have committed to cause such tears. He stews in his own juice, as it were. It's the microwave stratagem of attack.

But I was intrepid. And despite the explosions of my imagination, despite paroxysms of guilt in my belly, I would move forward to my third maneuver, which was to *accept* her attack so willingly that it would throw her off her balance. Guilty, was I? Guilty I would be.

"Okay, okay," I would cry with my hands up and my head down, the picture of remorse, "What did I do now?"

But all I got was crying.

Which left me mindless, frantic, and past control:

I would press her, and she would turn away.

I would touch her, and she would shrink from me.

I would stomp about the room to indicate immeasurable pain, cold loneliness, stark confusion, together with the fact that I had seventy pounds on her—

And finally she would cease her tears, finally look at me with blazing eyes and open her mouth—

And then poured forth such an ocean of wrongs, such a delineation of sins in such numbered and dated detail (whether I had intended any of them or not!) that I would stand shocked before the passion in one so short, plain drowning in her venom, aware that things had gotten out of hand, but speechless myself and very weak.

Well, then there was no help for it. I was forced to my final weapon and unapologetic for its power, having been so iniquitously

provoked. Without another word I'd jam my arms into my overcoat, bolt down the stairs of our little apartment, and pitch myself
into the cold St. Louis night, there to roam the sidewalks three
hours at a stretch, wondering whether our marriage would survive,
but confident that I had dealt guilt to Thanne's solar plexus and
had caused the desperate question in her heart of, Was I being
mugged?

Take that.

But then it happened that the Lord intervened, and one night
there should have been a different ending to the battle.

(But consider the camel.)

On that particular night (my birthday, as I remember, and
Thanne had strung that fact in large letters from wall to wall of
the living room, dear woman) we had followed the usual script of
our non-fights letterly, through solicitation, tears, pressure, tears,
stompings, undeserved accusations and the basset hound look in
my face, and tears—

Indeed, all went well, right up to the jamming of my arms
into the overcoat, the running downstairs, and the dramatic leap
into the night. But then God piddled on the affair.

When I slammed the front door, I caught my coat in it.

Mad and madder, I rifled my pockets for the key, to unlock
the damn door, to complete this most crucial tactic against Thanne's
peace of mind. Take—

But there was no key. My tail was truly in the door, and the
door was made of oak.

I had two alternatives. Either I could shed the coat and pace
the night unhoused, unprotected. There was real drama in that,
a tremendous statement of my heart's hurt—except that Thanne
wouldn't know it, and the temperature was below freezing.

Or else I could ring the doorbell.

Ten minutes of blue shivering convinced me which was the more expedient measure. I rang the doorbell.

So then, my wife came down the steps. So then, my wife peeped out. So then, my wife unlocked the door—and what was she doing? Laughing! Oh, she laughed so hard the tears streamed down her face and she had to put her hand on my shoulder, to hold her up.

And I could have smiled a little bit, too. I could have chuckled a tiny chuckle; for this was the gift of God, arranging armistice, staging reconciliation between a wife and her husband, a gift more sweet than all the rains of heaven. Laughter: extraordinary forgiveness!

But what did the dummy do? Well, he batted her hand away, cried "Hmph!" and bolted to stalk the night more grimly than ever before. *Then* he should have wondered about the survival of his marriage, not by fights distressed, but by his stupid, blind, inordinate, and all-consuming pride.

For he had denied the manipulations of the Deity.

Oh, learn from the dummy, ye husbands and wives, ye children and parents, ye politicians so often so unbending from your former policies. Learn, all ye who suffer fallings-out with one another and ye whose inclination is to lick your wounds in cold proud isolation! God doth constantly prepare the way for reconciliation, even by his gimmickry, if only pride don't blind you to the opportunity.

Edification/Demolition

TWO GAS STATION ATTENDANTS.

One met at a self-service pump, the other at her desk.

The first in rain on a chilly night. The second in the afternoon, but there was no sun in that building.

What caused their differing attitudes, I won't pretend to know. There may be a host of reasons why the latter attendant was so bitter, and much sympathy might be excited by each one. But that isn't the point, right now. Edification is the point, a Latin way of saying "building up." The power to build up other human beings, or else to tear them down, no matter how menial the circumstance nor how quick the meeting—that is the power possessed by each member of the Body of Christ, and a mighty power, indeed.

———◆———

I had my collar up against the rain. I hunched at the rear of the Nova, had screwed the gas cap off, and was running gas into the tank. My hand was numb.

Beside me, suddenly, stood the attendant, his hands in his pockets. His presence was not rushing me because it was at peace. He said, "Hello," and a smile flicked across his face. Nor was he some chill stranger, though I did not know him. When he spoke he looked directly into my eyes—without fear, without embarrassment, with neither judgment nor haughtiness nor threat. I, whoever I happened to be; I, whatever my family or my profession; I was there for him in that particular moment.

He was lean. Dark hair streaked his forehead with the rain. He shook his head slowly when he saw the brown face of my kid looking out the window, and raindrops spilled from his chin. I think he laughed. The fill-up seemed to take a long time.

Now, I ran on no crisis then. I hit seventeen bucks on the penny, capped the pipe, handed him the bills and watched while he folded them into his roll. He did not solve some terrible trouble of mine. Nor did he save me from disaster or fix some thing I couldn't fix. Nevertheless, this attendant did the extraordinary.

He shook my hand.

He smiled one more time, and to *me* he said, "Thank you."

I admit it: this is a minor and nearly forgettable incident. And it should be unworthy of book-print. Except that when I slid back into the Nova, I stopped a moment before turning the key, and Thanne said, "Why are you smiling?" Drip, drip, and a slowly spreading smile.

The fellow had built me up. He had edified me.

I never saw him again.

———◆———

Neither did I ever see the other attendant again. But I remember her, too.

She kept her separated seat while I filled my thirsty car. No matter to that. Most attendants don't pop out of the station for every Jack that jerks the handle. But when I entered the building, still she kept the seat and her eyes she kept downward, gazing at the top of her desk. There was no book there. She was not reading. She was simply staring.

I held out my money.

"Whadda-ya want me to do with that?" she said.

"Well, take it," I said. "I'm paying for the gas—"

"So how much was it?"

"Seventeen—"

There were lines from her nose to the corners of her mouth. Sullen lines. Anger, from some reason or other. And I was, it seemed, an intrusion in her life. She snapped the bills from my hand and bedded them in the slots of her register. She was chewing gum. It cracked like biddy-whips. She was whorling her hair with a forefinger.

I stood there too long, I think. She said, still without looking at me, "Your car stuck? You waiting for something?"

"No."

I slid disquieted into the car and sat a while. Demolition.

Sadness had made me sad. The day had been torn down utterly.

———◆———

You say: "But how can I serve the Lord? I'm not important. What I do is so common and of little consequence. Anyone can do what I do."

But I say to you: "Every time you meet another human being you have the opportunity. It's a chance at holiness. For you will do one of two things, then. Either you will build him up, or you will tear him down. Either you will acknowledge that he *is*, or you will make him sorry that he is—sorry, at least, that he is *there*, in front of you. You will create, or you will destroy. And the things you dignify or deny are God's own property. They are made, each one of them, in his own image."

And I say to you: "There are no useless, minor meetings. There are no dead-end jobs. There are no pointless lives. Swallow your sorrows, forget your grievances and all the hurt your poor life has sustained. Turn your face truly to the human before you and let her, for one pure moment, shine. Think her important, and then she will suspect that she is fashioned of God."

How do you say Hello? Or do you say Hello?

How do you greet the strangers? Or do you greet them?

Are you so proud as to burden your customer, your client, your neighbor, your child, with *your* tribulation? Even by attitude? Even by crabbiness, anger, or gloom?

Demolition!

Or do you look them in the eye and grant them peace?

Such are the members of the Body of Christ, and edification in a service station.

To Talitha, at Her Confirmation

I.

"TALITHA! TALITHA!"

The tone of that cry, both yearning and terrified, is what I most remember from this experience—that and the final comment with which Talitha ended it all.

"Talitha!"

It went to my soul immediately. But is was my son Matthew who was shrieking at his sister, urging her to get inside the gates.

"Oh, please, *Talitha!*"

———◆———

From the first pop, like a firecracker or a stick striking a picket, all motion suddenly slowed, as though events had begun to dance deep in a greening sea. Another pop went off outside the house, and then the screaming started.

Thanne said, "That's a gun."

Two years earlier I would have disputed her. The sound would have seemed too innocuous. And who would have been shooting in daylight, thirty minutes after the children had come home from school? The world was too bright and ordinary for gunfire. But I walked to the front window, drew back the curtains, and looked into the street.

Everything outside was, indeed, thick with a mortal circum-spection—and I saw a spurt of flame as orange as a number two pencil, and I heard the third pop, and there was a fat woman at the curb directly before our house, her mouth smeared in scream-ing, her right hand waving the pistol of peppery flame.

I whispered, "Oh, Thanne!" How could the world, how could the world. . . .

I leaped for the front door. I tore it open, leaped into the porch, then hung on the steps. Two events were unfolding slowly, each with an idiot's script and danger. Two people were scream-ing, one furiously, one fearfully.

The fat woman screamed in a perfect, self-righteous rage, purely careless of the neighborhood and any audience. She stood facing west down Chandler Avenue and stomping her great right leg: "Come back here! Come back here! You come back here, bitch, I kill you. Watch, watch, I be waiting for you!"

She put period to her threat by taking her fourth shot— *pop!*—wild down the street.

A second woman was running as fast as she could, her skirt riding high on her thighs, barefoot—the two shoes standing side by side behind her as if she had ascended angel-like leaving them neatly empty. This woman was not screaming.

My son was.

Matthew crouched half-hidden by the gate at the side of the house, his hands pressed to either side of his face: "Talitha!"

While his sister, my daughter, was standing on the sidewalk slope of the front yard, straight up, sucking a purple lollipop, and with innocent eyes watching this madness as if it were a movie. Nothing but a line of grass divided her from the shooting gun and this crazy woman.

Matthew knew the danger. His heart was failing on account of it, and he was paralyzed. Terrible was the anguish in his voice, because he loved his sister: "Taliiiiiiiitha! Run!"

But Talitha did not know the danger. She was not afraid. Ignorance, on the other hand, was no protection. Ignorance could kill her.

"Oh, please, Talitha!"

So I sailed from the porch and ran to the child. There was a fifth pop, but no pain. No bullet wound. Just an irritable tingling all over my flesh. Then what gave my little girl grief that day? What caused her to cry? I did, I guess, with snatching her up so suddenly, and bundling her roughly behind the gate, inside the fence and safety. Matthew stood gaping at the two of us, trembling like weeds in a high wind.

Talitha, when I set her on her feet again, deigned to give me a baby shove. She stomped one little foot.

"Daddy!" she scolded me, "you lost my lollipop! You," she paused, seeking her harshest accusation: "You ruined my whole day!"

Talitha. Oh, Talitha. You were five years old that day, already capable of a godlike blame.

2.

Today, Saturday the 3rd of May, 1986, you are twelve years and four months old. Talitha *duravisti!* Thou hast endured in spite of all, and thou art astonishingly lovely: *pulchra es, pulcherrima!*

You are nearly a woman, yes? The days of your independence are at hand. And you are my daughter; and you shall ever *be* my daughter, yes. But oh, how hard I had to work to earn this fatherhood and also to win for me your daughterhood. You do not, you need not—but I do and I must—remember.

————◆————

In one sense, the legal and the divine sense, you became our daughter the moment we adopted you in an Indianapolis courtroom. That covenant was binding from the beginning, requiring no knowing whatever on your part; for all the knowing, all the nourishing, and all forensic responsibility became your mother's and mine simply by our promising it. Like the grace of God, this covenant bore altogether upon us and not at all on you.

Binding, I say, as soon as the judge approved. Now no one could snatch you out of our hands. We clung to you as tightly as any mother clings to her children in a crowd: fiercely, protectingly, proudly, cutting a way for you through senseless and self-centered humanity, making a space in which you could dwell securely. You were ours by adoption, and we were yours by loving commitment.

But in another sense, the real and the relational sense, it took a long, long time to earn your willing daughterhood and to find my fatherhood in your eyes. I had to make a space for me in your heart. You see?

Your father I might be in fact; but it's a cold fact that is merely enforced and has no love in it. The legal covenant creates, as it were, a hollow house. This livelier covenant between us must bring that house to life and make a home of it. But that takes the exchanges of love. And love begins in trust. And trust begins in knowledge, and this second covenant, child, absolutely requires your knowing who I am in order to determine whether I am *worthy* of your trust. Worthy to hold your tender life in my two hands.

In a sense, then, I had also to be adopted by *you,* and that adoption had to be voluntary. No judge could decree it by saying: "The child shall hereby adore her father heart to heart, or said father shall have the right to bring suit against her in court, demanding affection by the power of the state. . . ." Surely, no parent is so juvenile as to *presume* love, or so mean-minded as to command it.

Well, and this parent never had the opportunity to be presumptive with you, Talitha. You exploded any such illusions at the very start, the moment you set eyes on me.

You do not, but I remember. . . .

I remember the day when the director of the adoption agency led Mom and me into a small, sunlit, institutional room to meet you, child. Upon entering, I saw a crib to my right. Within that crib lay a peanut, sleeping. Eight months old: your huge eyes closed and fringed with a rich black lash, your whole head shaped like a light bulb, soft scribbles of hair on the dome, your mouth a cupid's bow, your chin a diminishment. Girl, your color was a caramelized butter! And you were not so much snoring as making snozzle-noises in your nose—which shot me dead. I loved you straightaway and painfully.

So I bent my big frame down and brought my face low, closing the inches between us that I might smell your baby breath and next that I might kiss you.

What rests inside your slumbering mind? I wondered, balancing my sight between your well-etched eyebrows. Your birth-mother had initiated this adoption just two weeks ago; but she and all her decisions were as hidden from me as the dreams of sleepers are hidden from the wakeful. The agency said that you had begun to recognize the name this woman gave you (a name we did not know); for that reason they had hastened your placement.

By what name do you know yourself? And what sort of self, I wondered, dozed below me now?

I puckered. I was just about to mark your nose with the kiss of my fatherhood, when those huge eyes flew open. For just an instant you focused on my great, overhanging face; then your mouth grew wide; and then you screamed.

Oh, child, you screamed and screamed until I fell backward, out of your vision. Then you sobbed, staring wide-eyed everywhere around the room, and I knew! I knew you were looking for some familiar thing, some familiar, consoling human—but we were all strangers, and you were alone, and utterly strange to *me* was any image you held in your mind as a touchstone of peace and food and home and wholeness and security. I had no idea what parental countenance you could not find among us. I could not help you. I was helpless, and this was the pain of my love.

Thanne could help, though.

This new mother went to you and gathered you from the crib unto herself, and you wrapped your arms and legs around her as though never to let her go, and so your sobs subsided. And so, as we drove home from Indianapolis to Evansville, you sometimes drifted; but you never let go of your mother.

Thanne named you *Talitha*. She was thinking of Jairus' daughter, whom everyone said was dead, except that Jesus took her by the hand, saying, *"Talitha cumi"*—little girl, arise—and she arose and was hungry.

Even at home, even after weeks and then months, however, you didn't like me. No, let me be clearer: you were afraid of me. If I drew too near to you, your eyes widened and you held your breath a moment, and then you would break into the most desolated wailing.

When I preached on a Sunday morning and you, in your mother's arms, came to realize it was me, was my peremptory voice, wow! How you howled! And how swiftly the congregation ceased listening to me, listened to you, rather, and stayed daggers at me for troubling so sweet a child.

And sometimes you cried so hard you'd swoon. And the silence that followed your sudden faint was cavernous.

No, I could not presume your love. I could not command your trust. I was the father of the baby, but the baby's heart was kept from me; the baby's heart was filled with suspicion toward me; and I remained a stranger to the memories that still could trouble her. I knew her not, as she did not know me. Beauty cannot love the beast in the beginning. I was the father, but the baby was not yet my daughter.

I remember—

Once you backed bare-butt against the cold porcelain of the toilet, then jumped away as if it had been fire, shrieking in a genuine pain. But I could not comfort you (how filled with yearning I was to comfort you!) because I could not know the deeper cause of this wounding.

You were passive. So passive that for more than a year you did not play as other babies play.

Thanne remembers—

Your mother remembers the day she left you in the living room alone and went into the kitchen. Suddenly, out of the silence came a tinkling sound. Mom recognized that sound: a toy, a plastic ball which rang small chimes when it was rolled. Ah, Talitha, your mother ran to the living room door, then paused and felt the tears rising behind her eyes. *You* had pushed that ball! For the first time since coming to us, you had initiated a little game of your own. You were playing.

In precisely this way, love watches. Nothing escapes the eyes of love and the mind that might make sense of what it sees. For to be loved in return, love must earn the child's trust; and to earn trust, love must first learn the child's language, to speak in the language she knows.

And so I remember—

I remember one evening when the whole family sat at supper, Matthew round the corner to my right and Mary beyond him, Joseph round the corner to my left and you in your highchair by him with Mom beside you. Your face and that beautiful head were covered with a vegetable smear. You were doing some glad thing, like kicking your feet beneath the tray. And then, by merest chance, we glanced at each other, you and I, at precisely the same instant.

And you spontaneously lifted your eyebrows.

Love watches!

The love in me responded in kind: I lifted my eyebrows exactly as you had, to the same angle and the same expression.

You gaped. You never turned your eyes from me, but slowly, assessingly, you raised those well-etched brows again—while I mimicked the move.

You made your eyebrows leap. And I, with mine, took flight!

Oh, Talitha, you grinned at me then. I had learned the language. Eyebrow language. And I could speak it with flair, for next I raised a single eyebrow, and you rewarded me with a belly laugh!

Soon we were telling jokes to one another, whirling our brows, sending signs like semaphores. "What's that stuff on your face?" I said. And you said, "It ain't for eating!" And we laughed. "How are you?" I asked more sincerely. "Are you well, my child?"

And before we were done, with my eyebrows I said, "I love you."

And you with yours responded, "I know."

It was, perhaps, another year before you offered me your cupid's kiss, by which you said, "I love you, too." But in the meantime you let me touch you and hug you and feed you and talk with you and learn your mind and make that space within your heart.

3.

So there came the day when you trusted me to save you from dangers you yourself had not perceived. (Of *course* I'd never let that blood-lusty woman shoot you, girl!) Yes, and you trusted me so much that you could scold me without fearing to lose me. ("Daddy!"—stomping your pretty foot—"you ruined my whole day!")

And now has come the harder day . . .

———— ◆ ————

Cheap love, cheaply given and lightly received, cracks in the crisis. It isn't built to bear the weight. But expensive love, carefully sold

and dearly bought, grows like the oak. The crisis cannot break it
down. This is our love, Talitha.

Tomorrow, the last of our four children, you will speak publicly your independent faith in the Lord Jesus Christ. *You* do this
thing, not I; it is your initiative, not mine—though I have long
prepared you for it. You will use the language of adults, and none
shall speak for you; and those who listen, besides your mother
and me, are the greater community on earth, and the communion
of saints in heaven—and God. No longer do you move oblivious
of the enmity around you; nor need you mistake whom to trust
and thereby whom to love hereafter. It must be the One who best
knows the images and the secrets of your heart, He who has saved
you from sin and from death itself and from the Devil.

But still, love watches. My love, I mean: I will watch with joy
the continuing acquaintance you are making with yourself and
your growth; I will watch with an unexpressed trepidation the
boldness that must pitch you forward. . . .

It is a happy crisis, tomorrow, but a crisis nonetheless, when
the child leaves childhood and her home. It will change the both of
us—for how much of parenthood is left to me, when the youngest
finally takes her leave? I'm like you in your infancy: I want to cling
to you, Talitha. I want to keep my old values, my old worth (with
such difficulty proven to you) by clinging to the old you here.

Yes, but neither one of us is an infant now.

And I will not cling.

Because you, my strong daughter, have endured. *Talitha, duravisti!* And because our oaken love can still continue to grow and to
change as it has changed through the last twelve years. Love, as
slowly learned and earned as ours, is durable too. It can develop
into its own adulthood.

And what beauty, Talitha, you shall shed on the world, now
that you go unshadowed by me! O *pulcherrima!* Most beautiful,
beautiful daughter of mine! Go in peace.

And Through the Night
Watch O'er Your Beds

SARAH MOREAU MAKES A DIGNIFIED, unfaltering presentation of herself. Not that the woman is, in fact, so self-confident; nor that she is aggressive in her level-eyed look at you. Her voice is as soft as raiment. And she will admit, in moments of utter privacy, to a personal sense of inequality before the natural shocks of this world. But the pride in her eye is the little territory that she has marked for herself and for her family within this world, and is her means for meeting it. It's something like the wall around a city: a needful and altogether proper defense. But it is neither hypocrisy nor estrangement in Sarah. It *is* Sarah.

Therefore, when Sarah left the church, one Sunday morning, unable to raise her eyes to mine, when her face gave the appearance of weakness and wilt, I felt the difference deep in my chest. The walls were down, and that from the inside.

I touched her shoulder to indicate that it was no little question, and asked, "How are you?"

She said, "I don't think I can handle it," as though I knew what *it* was.

I said, "Will you come talk with me?"

She shivered and said, "Yes."

Three days made no change. As handsome as this woman is, light-skinned, grey-eyed, a broad forehead and a perfect widow's peak, she sat sunken in her sorrow, and the tears were not lovely; she apologized for them.

She had spent a month with her daughter in Atlantic City, she told me. Justine was dying of cancer, a child of thirty-eight years and beautiful to her mother's heart. Yet, as grievous a trial as that was for Sarah, there was a deeper grief—the *it* she could not handle.

This: Justine had not yet acknowledged what Sarah knew; the child was still clinging to life. So there had been a moment, before Sarah returned to Evansville, when she sat on the sofa holding her daughter, her daughter crying, "Help me," and Sarah so full of the things that she *wanted* to say, words of love and completion, but which she could *not* say because Justine was unprepared to hear them: the mother's heart was bursting from within, and the walls, which always held the enemy without, cracked before the internal attack, and all she could do was to cry in her helplessness, "I'm here. I'm here. I will always be here—"

And to me dear Sarah said, "Nobody wants to name the terrible thing. But I don't think I can do this alone."

"Well," I said, "now there are two of us, and these ears will hear you." And it seemed to me that a long and double-filed gauntlet stretched out in front of us, and so we prayed.

But I was wrong.

See how speedily, how impossibly quickly the cruel events can run, once they have begun. On Friday of that same week, Bram called me to say that his and Sarah's daughter had decided to come home, both she and her husband; and once she was settled, her husband would return to Atlantic City. But Bram couldn't say, "Come home to die." He busied himself with the details, and he sighed often.

On Saturday I visited the mother and the father in their home, and she was silent before the thing to come, and he was restless, and I said, "Please, please, let Justine direct you: don't impose on her either your sorrow or your anger or your painted and strained happiness. Listen to her. Find out where she is at, then measure your own expressions according to hers. Do you understand? This is her moment, her time. Do you understand?"

"I'll be her servant," said Bram. "I'll cook whatever she wants. I'll wash her. I'll make her bed. She'll be the princess. I wish I knew how to get her from the St. Louis airport. Well, I'll rent a van. She'll be glad to be home. She won't have to lift a finger—"

Sarah bowed her head silently.

On Monday Justine came into Evansville.

By Tuesday she'd been admitted to the hospital in order for the local oncologist, they said, to make his own determinations before she was released to home; and most of the family had gathered by then, two of her sisters from Louisville—Irene and Eve—and a brother, Peter, and children, her three sons; and on Tuesday I saw her for the first time, and her husband Herman. I went to Deaconess with the elements for Holy Communion, and the air was thick with difficulty, and I wondered severely about my own strength—

———◆———

In the first chapter of John, the last verse of that chapter, the Lord Jesus Christ makes a promise unto his fresh-faced disciples. It is a promise that seems to lean upon the Old Testament for interpretation, and therefore draws its shape and its reality out of the past; and though promises by nature focus on the future, this one is so backward-looking that its future remained for me unfocused. For myself, I could not grasp what goodness Christ was offering.

"You shall see greater things than these," says Jesus. "Truly, truly, I say to you, you will see heaven opened, and the angels of God ascending and descending upon the Son of man."

It's a marvelous prediction. It echoes Jacob's experience at Bethel. And since it places the Son of man at the bottom, while we remember that the Presence of the Lord God was at the top of the ladder of messengers, it seems to be a characterizing promise—one solely directed to Jesus, identifying him and given to us for our instruction, but *not* one given to us as actual beneficiaries of the promise. It seems to say, "By this you will know," and not, "you will yourselves receive." Thus, it seems a closed-circuit sort of promise between the Father and the Firstborn, and we get to look on. That's all. The image of ascending and descending angels is so symbolic—so much a backward allusion—that I could apprehend no reality for it in my own experience and in my future. It could be a doctrine of mine. But how ever could it be for me a breathless expectation, with these two eyes to see it?

So, I thought casually, don't be Nicodemus with these words, demanding fleshy what the Lord meant spiritually. You'll look the fool and you'll reveal a dreadful lack of insight.

But twice the Lord said "See" after he himself had given a demonstration of seeing, "seeing" Nathanael under the fig tree, "seeing" the guileless character of this Israelite by spiritual eyes, to be sure, yet with fleshy and factual objects for his sight. Such "seeing" was not divorced from experience. Rather, it saw and then saw more deeply the true nature of experience. Thus, spiritual insight was not "other than" fleshy sight, but "through and through" it, interpreting it!

Why couldn't I expect, then, to "see" these angels, if not in my experience, then *behind* it? Ah, but how, how, with a promise so vague?

Moreover, the Lord's promises in John are never to be taken lightly; nor are they kept in a merely instructional or doctrinal manner, something to be learned, as it were.

Does he promise the Holy Spirit? Well, and then he gives the Holy Spirit by the experiential event of a resurrection appearance, and a breathing upon disciples, and a clearly evidential *changing* of them. A spiritual occurrence, to be sure; but not one invisible to the eyes of flesh.

Does he promise peace unlike the giving of the world's peace?

Well, and then in the same appearing he makes good his promise and delivers unto them his peace.

Likewise, joy.

Likewise, "I will come to you."

In John, promises find their fulfillment, are *not* forgotten. And in John that fulfillment is inclusive (not just between the Father and the Son, but also involving the disciples) as well as transfiguringly real (and not just spiritualized to a teachment).

So: then where did I come in? And how would *I* see the angels?

A friend of mine, an exegete named Robert Smith, helped me. He pointed to a possible remembrance of this first promise of Jesus, one that followed the same pattern of promise-keeping as I've touched above, because it came post-resurrection, was inclusive, and was fleshy sight on its way to spiritual insight. And when I looked at this keeping of the promise, I found not just the backward allusions to Jacob, but the configurations of experience that I myself knew and could know in the future; I saw the fleshy objects of seeing, common details, through which, by the grace of God, I might hereafter "see" angels!

Bob pointed to what Mary Magdalene saw, but could not yet see *through*:

"But Mary stood weeping outside the tomb, and as she wept she stooped to look into the tomb; and she saw two angels in white, sitting where the body of Jesus had lain, one at the head and one at the feet."

Ascending and descending upon the Son of man.

"They said to her, 'Woman, why are you weeping?' She said to them, 'Because they have taken away my Lord, and I do not know where they have laid him.'"

No knowledge, yet, that these are angels. No, not until Jesus himself calls her by name and sight turns to insight, flesh *through* flesh to spiritual truth, and death to resurrection, desolation unto joy.

But listen: whereas I hardly know Jacob's experience, I do most certainly know the experience of Mary Magdalene! And though I've never slept with my head upon a stone, I *have*, dear God, stood in places of death and have myself been riven with sorrow, blinded by it, broken by the loss. These details I know by the bone. Now, don't you see, the promise takes on the flesh it must have ever before it reveals unto me its Truth, its spirit. Now it finds focus in *my* future, too. O Mary Magdalene, you are my sister; I know where to look!

Bob Smith, dear friend of mine, I have a good thing to tell you.

Though not at the head and the foot, but rather on the left side and the right, I have seen the angels. Seen them, and after that, "seen" them deeply, and I was blessed.

———◆———

Justine turned and turned in her hospital bed. She kept drawing her knees to her chest, then thrusting them down again as if the first motion had stabbed her. This aggravated the catheter and the I.V. But she was in pain.

She was wasted. The skin was sunken at her temples; her cheeks were scooped to her teeth. Her eyes were thick with a milky, occlusive rheum. No. No. Sarah was righter than any of them: Justine was dying.

Bram said, "Well, how does she look to you?" A bright, heroic gambit. "Isn't that some girl of mine? Oh, she's a fighter, all right."

Eve, the youngest of them all, was close to tears. She was trying to explain herself to Justine, leaning over the bed. "I'm only trying to help you," she said. "You know that I love you."

Because Justine had said to her, "Don't worry me, girl."

But the girl was worrying her.

Her husband grinned when he met me, reminding me of a sermon I had preached a thousand years ago and acting like a gracious host in his own living room. He hadn't shaved. Improbably, since we didn't know each other well, he hugged me and hung on—but was grinning again at the release. "Do you want some coffee?" he said.

Sarah sat silently by.

I told them that I had brought communion for Justine. Could I give it to her now?

Sarah said to Herman, "Do you mind?"

Herman blinked at her, a blank surprise in his eyes.

"No," he whispered, and he left, although he was the husband.

Only later did I learn that he thought she was asking him to leave, and later he said, "Why wasn't I wanted there? What's the matter with me?" But that isn't what Sarah had meant at all.

The air was thick with difficulty. The healthy were having a horrible time even talking to one another, because disease had changed the world completely.

Whether Justine could understand me or not, I spoke to her as though she could. I explained that I would dip a tiny fraction of bread into wine, then put it upon her tongue, and this would be Jesus come into her, for strength, for faith, and for consolation. I said that she could pray with me in her mind. And then I prayed.

Kneeling beside the bed, while she twisted and others agonized about whether to hold her still, I spoke the words of institution, and I gave thanks (O Lord, what a mockery!), and I broke the bread, and I damped it with wine, and I held her poor head, and I touched the fleck of body to her tongue.

Suddenly she went still.

I was so grateful.

And then I was grieved.

For what she did, she considered this intrusion in her mouth. And then she rolled her tongue round and round, and she scraped the sticky bread from her jaw, and again and again she thrust it forward, but she hadn't the strength to spit. She didn't want it!

With a failing heart, I explained to the family (but what did I know of the mysteries?) that even if she hadn't swallowed, yet she'd eaten of the Lord's Supper; and sadly, with my forefinger, I scoured her mouth and brought the bit out again, and there it stuck to my flesh, and what was I to do with it then? Wash it down the drain? But it was the body of the Lord. Eat it myself?

The air was so thick with difficulty. Death damns all our healthy habits.

"Auuugh," moaned Justine, and there was Herman again.

He put his ear to her mouth. He understood that she was thirsty. And then this man who hid behind his grin effected a communion where mine had seemed so ineffectual.

He sucked water himself from a straw. He kissed his wife. She held still. This was a holy kiss, for he fed her water, and this she drank.

Now his own face broke.

"Can't you do something for her?" he pleaded with the nurses. "She's hurting. She's hurting so bad."

They gave her morphine.

The poor woman relaxed.

There were moments on Wednesday when she opened her eyes and spoke clearly. Everyone rejoiced in these moments, and they told them, word for word, to one another. They squeezed them for every drop of hope that wasn't in them. I came to pray, and in the visit heard of Justine's extraordinary progress. "She slept last night." "My girl's a fighter. She's rallying. Would you believe it? She said, 'Don't worry me, Papa.' She said, 'You kiss me one more time and I'll beat you.' So, I'm listening to her, just like you said." "She wants her nails done." This was Eve. "Don't you think we should do her nails? She always liked the way her hands look."

Whether she heard my prayers, I didn't know.

Whether she accepted the blessings that my hands put upon her forehead, I didn't know. What good was I in this place? I didn't know.

Late, late Thursday night—no, two A.M. on Friday morning—Justine died.

———◆———

All Thursday she lay in a coma, with her eyes open.

I declare unto you that when I came to her that evening, she was beautiful. The irises and the pupils were clear, now, though seeing nothing we could see. The deep brown flesh of her face had taken every depression of bone; and with her mouth ajar, as though at the first part of a word, she seemed like nothing so much as a saint of the early church, aggrieved by a treacherous pain, yet holy and otherly in her peace.

She was so thin. She was sticks arranged beneath the blankets. I could tell that she was breathing only by the pulsing underneath her jaw.

Sarah sat in a chair to her left. Something was wrong. The woman's silence was angry and her lips were pinched.

Bram, too, was silent, now—his back to the wall. He couldn't sit. And Herman constantly came and went. Peter was in the lounge, working on penciled figures, a Sony Walkman at his ears. He told me what was wrong. While Sarah was sleeping for a few minutes in the afternoon, Eve had followed instinct and the request that she'd heard Justine to make; she'd invited a manicurist into the hospital room who was only half-done with Justine's nails when Sarah returned. Sarah, then, was not pleased by the stranger's presence at such a personal affair, and tension flashed. Therefore, between Sarah and her youngest daughter, at this precious and terrible moment, there stood a wall, and the silence was hurtful to them both—and there was so little time left.

Difficulty. Dear Lord, the air was hard with it. And what was I to do? And how to open the gates between? And you, God—*where were you!*

They've taken away all the powers of healing in this world, and I don't know where they have put them—

When, past eleven o'clock, I returned to her room, Justine lay center in a little falling light. Right and left of her, each at a distance, were her father and mother, one against the wall and one in a chair by the curtain. Left and right of her, on the sides of the bed, holding her hands, were her sisters Irene and Eve—and the slender fingers of her hands and the deep red of her long nails were lovely beyond words. And I stood at the foot of the bed, hollow and unable.

But look at these sisters, and see what they were doing.

Eve had a linen handkerchief, with which she rubbed the tips of Justine's cuticles, over and over again; and I thought, What a ministration! The girl is serving the earthly need of her sister, even now making her beautiful, and how that must feel to Justine and what a comfort to know that this yearning need is being cared for when otherwise she might feel so unlovely! She's holding her hand; but she is also *serving* her in the grasp with a most peculiar love.

And—though she did not seem to mind whether anyone heard her or not—Irene was talking. Low, throaty, absolutely confident, Irene was speaking her faith.

"I know," she said, "that the Lord Jesus is in this place. I know he has not let you fall, Justine. I know the long, abiding love of our Savior for you, because I have felt it in myself—" For nearly twenty minutes Irene sang on and on in the ear of the dying, never a sob, never a broken note, but altogether assured.

And I gasped.

These were the angels! *These* were the ministers of the Lord, one accounting for an earthly need, the other for a heavenly one, moved unknowing by the presence of the Almighty, sitting side to side of a tomb going empty between them. I leaned far, far forward, not to miss a thing that the Lord was doing, nor a word of his love in Irene's mouth, and this is the time when I wept, but for gladness. He was not absent. He was here in these two. And I saw them fleshy at the loss, soft in the sorrow; but through them

I saw the descent and the ascent of the messengers of God and heard angelic motion toward a resurrection.

"Greater things than these will you see—"

I saw the love of God at work: "Rabboni!" I have seen the Lord.

———◆———

It is no small thing to say that then the difficulty of death passed out of the air, and I was free since I was no longer alone.

Both free and empowered, permitted to act.

Later, while I sat in the lounge, Eve came sobbing helplessly; no longer the angel in descent, she was simply a very sad daughter. I knelt before her and let her speak her anguish at a mother that seemed to have cut her off—the walls of emotion at death.

Then, soon after, I went back to the room where Justine lay and began conversation with Sarah.

"How are you?"

"I'm making it," she said.

"You're no longer shaken?" I asked.

She changed my word and answered, "No longer shaking. I can stand, now."

So I turned the talk. "This puts everyone to a strain, doesn't it?"

"Yes," she agreed.

"And it's easy to miss the living in the dead."

"Yes."

"Sarah, I think that Eve is very stretched out, just now."

Quietly, "Yes."

"Since you have the strength in you, now, would you watch for the chance to give this daughter some of your time and some of your love? She feels very lost, now, and maybe more lonely than you. She needs her Mama."

And then this is the truth.

Even while we still stood speaking, Bram and Eve came down the darkened hallway, and Bram was chattering of arrangements for the night, but Sarah moved immediately to her daughter and put holy arms of motherhood around her and held her tightly, tightly, and Eve wept with other tears outside her sister's room, and neither was alone any more.

Bram hardly knew what miracle was taking place. He kept talking of the arrangements. So I took his hand and walked him away from the two as though he were a child, and he came with me. It was a bold move on my part. But I could make it peacefully, now, because I knew—and I knew because I had seen it with my spiritual eyes—that God was in this place.

For hadn't I been promised that low, at the bottom of the ladder, in these circumstances, in the tears of death, would be the Son of man?

The Body of Christ—
Set Free!

FOR MOST OF THE JOURNEY, as we drove west and then west and finally south, our bus was filled with noise. We were a choir, after all, and young, and busy about ten concerts in ten days. Bus time was petcock time; we blew steam together.

But now the bus was silent. We were thoughtful and not a little frightened.

We were thirty-four bodies all together, a patchy collection of personalities, progressions, colors, classes and inclinations—though all of a single inner-city congregation and of the self-same Lord. Some were struck poetic by the Kansas sunset; others ignored it, singing songs of love in falsetto voices. Some nigh choked on the size of the Rocky Mountains and their whiteness; some stared at the heat gauge of the bus, anxious that the engine might overheat on a seven-percent grade; some ate; some slept; some played Uno and laughed; and the children did their homework, while others stayed oblivious, singing songs of love in falsetto voices.

Yet, for all our scattered concerns, our purpose was common and the same: through four states and eight cities we bore the Holy God upon our lips, his love in our voices—the Sounds of Grace, gone singing its Thanksgiving.

———— ◆ ————

Only now, on the afternoon of Thanksgiving Day itself, did all our moods become one mood, and we gazed forward grimly. Tense, silent, and uncertain. Songs of love had ceased. Falsetto throats had thickened. We were scheduled to sing within the Colorado women's penitentiary.

Holy, holy, holy. Who suckered us into this?

————•◆•————

"No pocket knives, no matches, no metal of any kind."

Thus we were instructed by one John Beltz, an admissions officer who had boarded the bus to direct us out of Canon City and then to authorize our entrance.

"No handbags, nail files, and no photographic film, because they can make bombs out of that."

Bombs?

"What kind of criminals are in this place?"

"All kinds," said John so airily, acclimatized, we supposed, to the scruff side of humanity. "Mostly lesser offenders, credit card fraud, prostitution. But there are murderers here, too. Infanticide, in the parlance. But don't worry. Passion-killers go quiet in prison."

But—

But we were to be the strangers in a strange, oppressive cage. We swallowed. And we worried.

Holy, holy, hold the throat of him who suckered us—

By no hand that we could see, the bars of the front gate slid open. Down a hall; past a glassed control center (guns there?); and into a waiting room set with tables and chairs, bright-colored like a restaurant. Here we met the Matron, a woman in plain clothes, smiling, respectful, and composed.

"The girls are free to listen to you or not, as they please. Line up in two rows, male and female. Raise your arms. Thank you."

One by one, male and female, we were patted down while our arms drooped out like chicken wings: pits, waist, back and stomach, crotch and legs. I was the first man frisked. The first woman came forward shivering as though she'd swallowed a raw and living fish. "Ohhh! That was terrible!"

Down another hall, fluorescent-lit, this time passed knots of women whose cigarettes hung at the lip, very few of whom returned our smiles. (Holy, holy—) They were slippered or barefoot (as they pleased?), undershirted, braless, or, at best, dressed in jeans and a flannel shirt. We struggled to act businesslike. "We've got good reason to be here." But we couldn't wipe the silly smiles off our faces. And we swallowed.

———◆·———

The auditorium was a great cement room in which all sound was as alive and clean as a guitar string. Folding chairs, a pool table, a huge wooden box (in which the piano was locked), and a little kindergarten stage.

Hollis began to set up the amplifier for his bass.

Brenda plinked at the freed piano.

There was some giggling and little humor.

Cheryl, louder than she intended, called the choir to position and to practice in its little space—

But who would listen to us? And of those who did, what would they care? Would they scorn us? Sneer in the face of our earnest offering?

Well, we were free to come and go. They weren't. That's a burdensome knowledge. We were soft as the civilized belly. These were hard, slouching and experienced. They walked like men and swore like mercenaries, with absolute, silken conviction. Yep: they could make bombs of film—and bullets out of toilet paper, for all we knew.

Cheryl raised her arms before our parti-colored choir, intending to practice a piece, to measure the sound of the place. Hollis hit a chord.

And then the stark wonder began.

———•◆•———

Sloppy was our singing at first, but very fast and punctuated by our clapping. Nerves are an excellent upper. "Good!" shouted Cheryl as voices came together. "Good!"

She hardly saw behind her an entering band of women, hard eyes gone curious—but Hollis did. By the fourth and the sixth contingent of the inmates' entrance, hot, black Hollis was smiling like he never had in church, and his guitar had discovered a new certitude, new rhythm that flirted with the unholy, holy, holy—

It wasn't even time, yet, for the concert to begin. No introductions had been made, either by voice or music, and this was *not* our program. Yet the women were coming, and the practice piece drew a spattering of applause, and Cheryl was lost. By fitful habit she led the choir into another piece for practice, "Soon and very soon, we are going to meet the king." Oh, the choir swung hard and speedily against its beat, and Timmy simply hid himself in the solo, and the women laughed at our abandon, and behold: the song itself, it took us over! The nerves left us, and we too began to laugh as we sang, as though there were some huge joke afoot, and we were grateful for the freedom in our throats, and we looked, for the first time, on one another, nodding, slapping another back, singing! And the women took to clapping, some of them dancing with their faces to the floor, their shoulders hunched, and they filled the place with their constant arrival, and some-when—no one knew when—the practice turned into an honest concert, but there was no formality to it, because we were free, don't you see, free of the restraints of propriety, free of our fears, free to be truly, truly one with these women, free (Lord, what a discovery!) *in prison.*

Song after song, the women stood up and beat their palms together. And they wept, sometimes. Timmy can do that to you. And at one point the entire auditorium, choir and criminals together, joined hands and lifted those hands and rocked and sang, "Oh, How I Love Jesus."

My God, how you do break the bars! How you fling open the doors that prison and divide us! This is true, for mine eyes have seen it and my heart went out to it: You are so mighty in your mercy.

The last song sung was not ours at all. Some thirteen of the inmates demanded that we sit while they took the stage. Then, in shaky voices and in nasal Spanish, embarrassed as schoolgirls but arms around each other for support, they sang:

"De Coloris! De Coloris! The sun gives its treasures, God's light to the children. . . . And so must all love be of every bright color to make my heart cry."

They sang, braless and holy, so holy: "Joyfully! We will live in God's friendship because he has willed it, pouring outward the light from within, the grace of our God, his infinite love—"

They sang. And we answered, "Yes." And the mountains themselves said, "Amen."